Bought by the Beast

A Dark Romance

Lexi Heart

Copyright

For updates and information on new releases and exclusive excerpts from her work, visit Lexi Heart at:

Website: https://www.lexiheart.com/

Facebook: https://www.facebook.com/LexiHeartAuthor/

Twitter: @LexiHeartAuthor

Gmail: LexiHeartAuthor@gmail.com

Instagram: @LexiHeartAuthor

Join my EXCLUSIVE Mailing List!

If you want to receive updates on new releases, special excerpts, and free stories, visit my website to join my exclusive mailing list!

https://www.lexiheart.com/

Bought by the Beast

Daisy

When my family gets deep into debt with the Russians, I sell the only thing I can to save them: my virginity. He may be able to take my body, but he will never have my heart. It's only a week. One week in the bed of the city's most notorious criminal. I can handle it. I have to. But I don't count on his scorching sensuality, his surprising sweetness. His fierce protectiveness. I know he's the last man in the world I should fall for, but his touch ignites something deep inside me. His dark, tormented soul calls to mine, draws me in, forces me to feel things I've never allowed myself to feel before…

Dmitry

Working as a hit man for the Russian Mafia, my life is nothing but an endless abyss of violence and solitude. My only goal is to keep my head down and do my job until I've repaid my debt and can get the hell out. I'm so close. Soon, I will be able to put this life of blood and death behind me. Until I see her. Daisy. Sweet. Innocent. With a core of hardened steel. Everything I've ever wanted, and everything I know I can never deserve. In a world full of darkness and cruelty, Daisy is like a ray of sunlight shining down into the pits of my personal hell. She is the light to my darkness, the innocence to my depravity. I will move heaven and earth to make her mine. And God help anyone who gets in my way.

** A full-length 67,000 word standalone, sizzling hot romance set in a dark landscape with no cheating, no cliffhanger, and a guaranteed HEA! This book involves explicit scenes, dark themes, and may contain triggers, but amid the violence and danger, two souls learn the true meaning of love and sacrifice. **

Chapter 1

DMITRY

I sit in silence and watch him slowly come back to consciousness. He's confused, as they always are. Next will be the questions.

"Where am I? How did I get here?" Freddy asks, his panicked gaze darting around the shadowy basement.

How predictable.

"Who helped you?" I ask, trying to keep the boredom from my voice.

"Helped me with what?"

I suppress a sigh. Why do they always make it so difficult?

The metal chair creaks as I stand and slowly straighten to my full height. Freddy shivers when he gets his first good look at me. I step closer, letting him look his fill. His gaze traces the white scars slashing across my face. I've already taken off my shirt in preparation for this grisly business, so he has an unobstructed view of the ugly marks crisscrossing my torso.

When his eyes finally lift to mine, he knows it's over. He doesn't have to ask who I am. My scars are notorious in our circles, as is my reputation. He knows he won't be leaving this dank room. Not alive. The only thing he can hope for now is a quick death. How much he suffers before that is up to him.

"You're… you're Vasilek's Beast. Oh, Jesus! I didn't do anything. I swear. Oh God! I didn't do anything!"

He struggles against the ropes binding his wrists behind his back, but it's useless. It's always useless. Even if he could get free, a man like him has no chance against a beast. Realizing this, he tries pleading again.

"Look, Ivan knows me! Call him, you'll see! There's no need to do this! I didn't—"

A sharp crack echoes through the room as the back of my hand connects with his face. I've heard enough. It's always the same. The begging, the pleading, the denying. It's exhausting. Doesn't he realize I wouldn't be here unless I already had proof? It's not a fishing expedition. I know exactly what he did. He could save us both so much time if he'd just admit it already.

"Who do you think sent me? I already found the bag of money under your sink. If you're going to plead innocence, you should have hidden it better. The only reason you're still alive is because I know you're not smart enough to pull it off by yourself. A nobody like you doesn't rob the Russian Mafia. Not alone. Not without help."

"No, I didn't—I swear! Someone set me up! I don't know anything about any money!"

I resist the impulse to rub my temples. They always have to make it so fucking difficult.

A swift strike to his solar plexus silences him mid-lie. He gasps, mouth gaping like a fish trying to breathe out of water.

The creak of the floorboards upstairs gives me pause. I pull out my Smith & Wesson and take aim at the empty doorway leading to the stairs.

A beat later, Josef appears, his blond hair shining even in the dim recesses of the basement.

Seeing my raised piece, he grins. "No one gets the drop on you, do they?"

"What took you so long?" I ask, holstering the weapon. "You were supposed to be here twenty minutes ago."

Hope sparks in Freddy's eyes when he sees Josef. Maybe he thinks he'll have a better chance of talking Josef out of killing him. As if either of us has ever let ourselves get talked out of finishing a job. Ivan Vasilek runs the southern part of Philly, and he pays us well for what we do. And even if he didn't, I owe that man my life. I could never betray him. Neither of us could.

"Got held up." Josef gives Freddy a wide smile, showing his teeth. The maniacal glint in his eyes has Freddy cringing back in the rickety metal chair. Josef loves a good interrogation.

"Did he say anything yet?" Josef asks, fiddling with his Glock, his eyes never leaving Freddy's.

"Not yet. But I found the money. Moron hid it under his sink. It's missing exactly half. He's working with someone, but he won't say who. Not yet, at least."

I turn away from Freddy's terror-stricken face to inspect the tools lined up on the battered wooden table.

"Please!" he cries, begging now. "I didn't do it! I was set up!"

I select a large sledgehammer, mentally turning my mind off. It's just a job. One that I'll be finished with soon. But damn, if these assholes would just make it easy, just once.

It's not like I get off on bashing in another man's kneecaps. They bring it on themselves. They could save me and themselves so much trouble if they'd just tell me what I want to know.

I swing the hammer experimentally, getting a feel for its weight. I doubt this sniveling wreck will last more than one whack. They rarely do.

Freddy's pleading cuts off as dull thuds begin echoing off the stone walls. Josef laughs, hitting him over and over, not giving him a chance to catch his breath, let alone talk.

Amateurs.

If you're going to beat it out of him, there's no use in exhausting yourself and cutting up your own hands. That's what tools are for.

At least Freddy's quiet now, except for the pained grunts and whimpers. I hate it when they beg. What's the point? He knows he's going to die. He can at least go out with a little dignity.

"Josef," I say in warning. Freddy's head is flopping back and forth with each strike, blood covering his face and Josef's hands. "He can't answer any questions if he's unconscious."

"He stole from the Boss. You caught him red-handed. Fucker. Has. To. Pay," he says between each strike.

"If you kill him before he answers our questions, his partner is going to be a lot harder to find."

Josef slows, then finally stops, breathing hard. His knuckles are torn, blood splattered across his face and neck. But that's nothing compared to Freddy's mangled face. One side is entirely caved in, jaw and eye socket shattered. The scent of copper hangs heavy in the stale air.

"Jesus, Josef. Is he still breathing?"

Josef crouches down and listens to his chest. "I think so."

"He's not going to be any use like this. Even if he does come to, he won't be able to speak."

"What do you want to do with him?" he asks.

In answer, I pull my gun from its holster and fire one shot into his skull. The sharp crack reverberates around the small basement, even with the silencer on.

"Get rid of him. We'll have to figure out another way to find whoever else was involved."

Josef doesn't bat an eye as he starts on the grisly task of cleaning up the blood and brain spatter. It's one of the reasons I don't mind working with him, despite his habit of reacting first and thinking second. He's one of the only people in Ivan's outfit who isn't afraid of me. At least, not much. He's as fucked up as I am; my scars are just more visible.

"So, did you do it?" I ask once the body is wrapped and ready for transport.

"Yeah, it's done. Gotta warn you though, Viktor's been asking questions about why we keep lending that scum bag more money. I managed to put him off for now, but if it keeps up much longer, he may decide to intervene himself."

"No need. He's in deep enough. Make sure he knows about the auction."

Josef grins. "Already mentioned it."

"Good." The tightness in my chest loosens just a little. It's all coming together.

"She's a pretty little piece, I'll give you that—"

"Stay away from her," I growl. "She's mine."

Any other man would piss himself if I used that tone of voice on him, but Josef just grins wider.

"Don't worry, D. I wouldn't tread on another man's territory. Especially yours. I'm just saying, you're putting an awful lot of work into this. Wouldn't it be easier to just ask her out?"

The tightness returns to my chest. Ask her out? Is he fucking kidding me? I square my shoulders and straighten my spine. I meet Josef's gaze and hold it, not saying a word.

I don't have to. Josef's eyes scan the scars on my face and body before he turns away. "Yeah, I guess not."

We finish cleaning the room in silence, eliminating every trace of us or the body. That's what Freddy is now. No longer a person, just a body to be disposed of.

As we work on the mindless task, I turn over Josef's words. Even if I could ask her out, a date isn't what I want. I want to own her. To utterly possess her. I want her on her knees, on her back, against the wall, and anywhere the fuck else I tell her to go. After tomorrow night, she'll be desperate to please me, eagerly obeying my every order. She'll be completely mine. And once I have her, she's never getting away.

After we finish, Josef heads out to dispose of the body and I head to the same place I go every night after work.

The neighborhood is full of rundown houses spaced too close together. Luckily, my goal is the small house at the end of the dead-end street. There are enough trees bordering the yard for me to disappear into.

It's quiet. Dark. No one else around. Just the way I like it. I sit in the shadows, waiting.

I hear her quiet footsteps on the sidewalk before I see her. Finally. She's home late tonight. I lean more heavily against the trunk of a tree, settling in to watch as she unlocks the front door and walks into the duplex.

I watch her through the window as she goes about her nightly routine. As soon as she's through the door, she's tidying up the house, cleaning the kitchen and washing dishes, even though she just finished an eight-hour shift at the shitty diner she works at. And even though her brother, mom, and her mom's latest boyfriend have probably been home all day, not one of her family members bothered to clean up after themselves. All of that falls on Daisy's shoulders, just like the burden of paying the bills to keep a roof over their heads.

Anger at her irresponsible family rises up, destroying the small amount of peace I've gained from being within shouting distance of her.

Her mom works, I remind myself. But her paycheck isn't enough to cover both her boyfriend's addictions and the bills. And the brother, as far as I can tell, is useless. At least he doesn't appear to be a junkie like the boyfriend, but as the elder brother, he should be doing his part to take care of his family, rather than relying on his mom and sister for everything.

Once the house is clean to her liking, she heads into her room and strips out of her waitressing uniform, eager to wash the grease and feel of other men's eyes off her body.

There's a tense moment when she freezes, hand going up to cover her chest. She peers at the window as if she heard a noise. She appears to look right at me, but I know she can't possibly see me. Still, the feel of her eyes on me causes my pulse to race in equal parts anticipation and trepidation.

What will she think of me, when she does see me?

It's a thought I don't like to ponder. When we finally meet, she'll have no choice but to be eager to please. I'll make sure of that.

She disappears into the bathroom. I take the opportunity to mentally review that everything is in place for tomorrow. It can't come soon enough.

She exits the bathroom, her wet hair tangling around her shoulders. My gaze traces her generous curves accentuated by the too-small towel.

I feel myself grow hard as I watch her pull on her tiny shorts and tank top. As she brushes out her golden hair, I imagine what it will feel like wrapped around my fist while she kneels in front of me, those plump, pouty lips opening for me, eager to suck me down.

Shifting my weight, I adjust the front of my jeans.

Now comes my favorite part. Once she's dressed with her hair pulled into a knot on top of her head, she sits down in front of the large easel next to the window. Sighing, I relax further against the rough tree and settle in.

She begins sketching, her delicate hand moving swiftly over the canvas. As she works, her entire demeanor transforms. Her shoulders straighten from their slumped, exhausted position. Her face calms, a look of peace and joy settling over her features. I feel my own restlessness fade, no match for the serenity on her face.

The night's events drift away like smoke, and it's just me and her, alone in the world. My chest loosens, allowing me to finally take a full breath. This, right here, is the only place I manage to find any peace.

I stand in the dark for hours watching her. I have no idea what it is she's drawing; my gaze doesn't leave her face. It doesn't matter anyway. Whatever it is, it's giving her a measure of happiness in her demanding, fucked up life.

Once I get my hands on her, I'll make sure she has nothing to worry about except pleasing me. I'll be doing her a favor, taking her away from this shitty house and her no-good family. I'll make sure she wants for nothing.

Unlike some men, I take care of what's mine.

Chapter 2

DAISY

"Lunch almost ready?" Jeremy asks, swiping a piece of the chicken I just fried.

I swat at him, but he dodges, his six-foot-frame more agile than it looks.

"Almost. You know, you could cook once in a while," I say as I turn off the burner and spoon the mashed potatoes into a bowl.

"Then what would you do?" He grins, eyes dancing.

I fight a smile. Damn him. My brother knows how to charm his way out of everything,

"Yeah, what would I do with all that free time?" I ask sarcastically.

Free time. What a novel concept. I don't think I've had 'free time' since I was in middle school. Maybe not even then. I work my butt off all week, every week. There's always something that needs to be done.

"Here it is." I plunk the food down on the kitchen table. He immediately pounces, eating like he hasn't seen food in a month.

"Make sure to leave some for mom!"

"Why? She won't be home for hours, and you know reheated fried chicken tastes like crap."

"Hours? What are you talking about? She had the breakfast shift today."

"Yeah, well, she called and said she's working a double."

"That's the fourth time this week. She's going to kill herself at this pace. Why is she doing so much overtime?"

"I heard her and Ray fighting last week. About money, again. I'm guessing he's running low, so she's pulling extra shifts."

"Of course he can't get off his ass and earn his own money," I grumble, throwing the pots in the sink.

" 'Course not. He never has before, why change now?" Jeremy says, helping himself to more chicken.

I scowl. I never understand how he can be so nonchalant about mom's boyfriends mooching off her like this. Then again, it's not like Jeremy works forty hours a week to help pay the rent like me. He doesn't understand the hard work that goes into earning the money Ray so blithely drinks away.

Despite Jeremy's charm, he can't seem to keep a job longer than a few weeks. He may be two years older than I am, but he's still a child in many ways.

"I need to get going or I'm going to be late. Please don't forget to wash the dishes this time," I say as I head out of the room. "I don't want to come home to a sink full of dishes again!"

"Yeah, yeah," he says, half listening, eyes already glued to his phone.

I roll my eyes and glance at the clock. Almost noon. Damn it. I'm going to have to jog the whole way to make it on time.

I quickly change into my ugly yellow waitressing uniform and rush out of the house.

"How'd you make out?" Samantha asks, brushing her bright red hair over her shoulder as she leans against the counter next to me. Sam is the same age as me. We both started working here around the same time when we were both still in high school. Over the years we've bonded over late night coffee and shitty family drama. Her home life is even more screwed up than mine. She's the closest thing I have to a friend.

"About sixty bucks," I say shrugging.

"That's it? Those guys at table five looked like they'd leave you a good tip."

I grimace as I print out the check for my last table of the night. "Yeah, they spent the whole time staring down the front of my shirt, then left me a lousy five-dollar tip. Assholes."

"Damn, that sucks."

"Yeah. Not my best night, but at least I'm out of here by eight tonight." I grin at Sam, knowing she's stuck until closing. I usually work the late shift with her, especially on the weekends, but today Max needed me to cover one of the earlier shifts for a girl who just up and quit without notice. Though the tips are considerably less for the early afternoon shift, I didn't complain when he asked me to cover. It's been weeks since I've been home earlier than midnight.

I can already feel the tension leaving me as I think about the hot shower waiting for me at home. And, even better, the hours and hours I'll have tonight to devote to my latest sketch. I've been experimenting with a new shading technique and can't wait to see the final product. My lips pull up into a smile just thinking about getting home and losing myself in my art. Since it's Friday, Jeremy, Ray and my mom will all probably be out. I'll have the house to myself for once. I can soak up the peace and quiet, something I rarely have the opportunity to enjoy.

"Well, enjoy your night," she says, smiling back. "I can't remember the last time you had a night off. Do you finally have a date lined up or what?"

I laugh as if she made a joke. "Yeah, just what I need—another person to feed and clean up after."

"Men have their benefits," she says with a sly smile and a wink.

"Right..." I roll my eyes.

After taking care of my last table, I retrieve my purse from the small locker and rush out the back door, eager to get home.

I take deep breaths of the cool night air, trying to block out the sound of traffic on the busy street. Philadelphia may not be that big of a city, but the traffic seems never-ending. Luckily, the diner I work at is on the outskirts of the busiest part of the city, only a few short blocks away from the tiny duplex we rent. I spend the time thinking about my sketch waiting for me at home. I picture the image in my mind, scrutinizing it from every angle. The drawing is one of my better ones, but it's still missing something. I mull it over during the short walk, and by the time I'm unlocking the front door, I think I've figured it out. I'm so eager to sit down and start working that it takes me a moment to realize the light in my room is on.

I stop in the doorway, momentarily confused. My belongings are strewn all over the place, the contents of my drawers scattered across the floor. My nightstand is knocked onto its side, the mattress from the bed is flipped, leaning drunkenly against the far wall.

My first thought is that we've been robbed—it wouldn't be the first time. A noise comes from the closet to my right, followed by a low curse.

My heart leaps in my throat. Someone's still in here. Then his voice registers. That familiar drunken slur...

"Ray?"

There's a loud thud, as if I startled him. He stumbles from the closet, his sunken face even more gaunt than usual.

"What the hell are you doing?" My gut burns with anger as the shock begins to wear off.

"Daisy," he grunts, eyes locking on mine. "Where is it?"

"Get out!" I take two steps toward him, furious. "Get the hell out of my room!"

This room is my sanctuary, the only place I can allow myself to relax, to let my guard down. How dare he come in here and tear it apart? How dare he violate the one place in the world I can call my own? If it weren't for me, we would have been kicked out of here long ago. This space is mine.

Without warning, he lunges at me, thin hands surprisingly strong as they wrap around my forearms. "Where's the money? Where is it!?"

I'm too shocked to react at first. He shakes me so hard my teeth rattle in my head. I try to twist out of his grasp, but he shoves me against the wall before I can break free.

Icy prickles of fear skate across the back of my neck. Some of mom's boyfriends have gotten physical in the past, but not Ray. He's a loser, sure, and a drunk, but he's never hit us. Not once. But the look in his eyes tonight…

I shiver. He stinks like a distillery, but his eyes are stone cold sober. But that's not what makes my blood run cold. It's the wildness I see there. The desperation.

"I know you've been saving up for that fancy school you're always going on about. I need that money. We need it. Where is it? Where?"

He shakes me again, fingers digging into my skin. Suppressing the knot of fear in my gut, I shove him away with as much force as I can muster. Surprise widens his eyes as he falls backward. His arms pinwheel as he tries to keep his balance, but his foot catches on the leg of the bed and he trips backward in the direction of my easel. I gasp, watching in horror as he crashes into it as if in slow motion. He may not be a large man, but my rickety easel is no match for his body weight. He crashes down on top of it in an explosion of splintered wood and shredded paper.

My heart freezes in my chest. Ray groans, seeming dazed, but it barely registers.

All my hard work is gone. Destroyed in the blink of an eye. Not just the sketch I've been working on for days, but the entire sketchpad, the easel, my special graphite pencils. All of it. Just gone, because of one drunken asshole.

I blink at the burning in my eyes, refusing to cry in front of him. I know it's stupid to be so upset over a few ruined drawings, some cheap pencils, and a simple wooden frame, but they were mine.

Most of the money I make goes toward paying the bills and putting food on the table. Every other week, I deposit a very small portion of my paycheck into a savings account I opened a few years back. I've been saving every cent I can, hoping to one day have enough to pay for some art classes at the community college. Back in high school, my grades were good enough that I might have been able to earn a scholarship if I had stayed. But in my senior year, one of my mom's boyfriends ran us into debt and took off, so I was forced to drop out and get a job in order to keep a roof over our heads. I've since earned my GED, and at twenty-one, I almost have enough saved to take my first college course.

Indulgences like sketch pads and graphite pencils are a luxury I can rarely afford. And now they're gone. My meager, but much prized, stash of art supplies has been completely obliterated by this drunken freeloader. He lives here rent free, steals my mom's money to pay for his drugs and booze, and now he's invaded my room and destroyed my most prized possessions.

My hands ball into fists. I dig my nails into my palms; the sharp sting focuses my anger and helps to keep the tears at bay.

Ray flops around on the floor, trying to right himself. I clench my teeth at the sound of snapping pencils and ripping paper beneath him. By the time he climbs clumsily back to his feet, I'm seething, all impulse to cry burned away in the face of my mounting fury. I clench my muscles, reigning in the impulse to launch myself at him.

"I need that money," he says again, oblivious to the hate filling in my eyes. "We're in trouble. I fucked up. We're dead. Fuck—we're all dead…" He yanks on his graying hair, eyes wild.

Slowly, his words pierce the red haze of anger surrounding me.

"What are you talking about?" My voice quavers the tiniest bit as anxiety blooms in my chest.

"I fucked up," he says again, slurring slightly. "I owe some money. If I don't pay up, they'll kill us. They'll kill all of us." He slumps down on the ground, defeated. "I was gonna win big, I swear. I only needed a little loan, and I was gonna double that money. It was a sure thing! A fixed race—I got a tip. But the bloody horse lost! It's all gone! And now, if I can't pay Vasilek back by the end of the week, he'll make examples of all of us…"

The blood drains from my face. "Vasilek? As in Ivan Vasilek? The Russian mob boss?"

He nods numbly. "If I can't pay, he'll send his men to kill us."

My hand fumbles behind me for the wall. I lean back against it, my mind spinning.

He borrowed from the Russians…. My God… What was he thinking?

"How much?" I ask. "How much did you borrow?"

"Twenty thousand."

The number is mind-boggling. No wonder he's been pressuring my mom to work doubles all week. But even if we sold everything we own, we'd never be able to pay that amount back.

Oh, my God. They're going to kill us…

"We need to leave." My legs tingle, the center of my chest ringing hollow. "We need to run," I say more forcibly. "Tonight. Before they come looking for us."

He's shaking his head before I even finish, still slumped on the ground. "Wouldn't do any good. They probably already have someone watching the house."

"Well, we have to try something! We can't just sit around getting drunk like you!"

It's always astounding to me how my mom could get involved with such scum bags over the years. How she could stay with men who treated her and her kids so badly. I love my mom, but I can't help resenting her, too. Ray is just the latest in a string of horrible men she's dated over the years. And now, because of her crap choices and Ray's idiocy, we all might end up dead.

"Well..." He glances up at me with a look I know well. It's the look he gets when he's about to manipulate my mom into giving him more money or another chance before she kicks him out. "There is something you could do...if you wanted to."

"Ray, even if I gave you my entire college fund, I wouldn't be able to pay that large of a debt. Christ, we could sell the car and still wouldn't get half that!"

"There's another way..."

I raise an eyebrow, waiting.

"The Den of Iniquity is holding an auction tonight."

"What does that have to do with me?"

"They're auctioning off women. One of Vasilek's guys told me about it. He said a pretty thing like you could make a fortune there; more than enough to pay the Russians back. You'll probably even have a little money left over when all is said and done. Maybe even enough to pay for those classes you've been talking about."

My jaw clenches. He can't be serious. "You expect me to pay off your gambling debt by selling my–selling my body–" I stutter, horror washing over me at the thought.

"It's just sex," he says, like prostituting myself out is no big deal. And for him, it's probably not. I'm sure he's done much worse things over the years to get his next fix. "Do you have a better way to get twenty grand by tomorrow?"

Tomorrow? There's no way. It's impossible.

"Can't you ask for an extension? If we had another week, maybe we could…" I trail off. Even with another week, how on earth would I get that much money?

"The Russians aren't exactly forgiving when it comes to gambling debts. If I don't have the money tomorrow, they'll kill us. Not just me. They'll kill you, your mom, Jeremy, all of us."

He's right. Though I've never been involved with them directly, I've heard things about the Russians. They're hard and cruel and ruthless. They aren't the kind of men you want to cross. They will kill our entire family just to make an example of us.

The backs of my eyes prickle uncomfortably. I blink it away. Now isn't the time to feel sorry for myself. My mom's and brother's lives are at stake.

"What time is the auction?"

"We have to leave in a half hour to make it on time."

I hesitate, heart pounding in my chest. But he's right. There is no other way.

"Alright. I'll do it."

Ray sags in relief. "Thank God. Quick, get in the shower and wash that diner grease smell off. You need to look your best if you're going to earn enough to pay them off."

My stomach rolls sickeningly. The first time I have sex is going to be with some old, rich pervert who buys me off an auction block…

"And make sure to pack enough for a week."

"A week?" My stomach drops.

"You don't think anyone would spend that much just to use you for one night, do you?"

Chapter 3

DMITRY

The crush of people is unnerving. It's been a while since I've been in a crowd this large. Looking the way I do, I tend to avoid people when I can. As if my height and large frame don't stand out enough, my scars certainly do. I work my way through the crowd, all my senses on overload. Luckily, most people stumble away from me once they catch sight of my ruined face, clearing a path towards the back.

The auction is slated to begin soon, but first I have to fill Ivan in on last night.

The private area in the back of the room is roped off from the rest. Ivan is there waiting for me, but he isn't alone. His son, Viktor, is sitting with him, and it looks like they're having another heated debate.

The bodyguard nods to me and unhooks the velvet rope to let me pass. Several more men are standing in a semi-circle around him, all on high alert. Ivan doesn't usually attend gatherings this large either, though for a different reason than my own.

As the head of one of the largest organizations in the tri-state area, Ivan has many enemies. You can't be too careful these days. Not now that news of Ivan's poor health has gotten out. I'm sure that's why Freddy thought he could steal from us. Like sharks, the city's criminal underworld smells blood in the water. With Ivan still recuperating from his illness this past winter, the other crime families in the area think we may be weakening.

But they underestimated us. They should never have used someone as dumb as Freddy to carry out their plans. Following his trail to the stolen money was child's play. Too bad Josef broke his jaw before I could find out who else was behind it.

Viktor scowls when he sees me approach. "I just don't see why you are so against it," he grumbles to Ivan. "It would increase our profits tenfold! The Bratva in Chicago has been in the business for decades, and look how powerful they are!"

"And the Chicago Bratva is now on the radar of every cop and fed in the country," Ivan says. Viktor opens his mouth to protest, but Ivan slams his fist on the table. "Enough. I've made my decision. We make more than enough with our other businesses. And I even allow you to have your little auctions here occasionally to keep you happy, so long as the women are willing. But we do not deal in human trafficking. I don't care if every syndicate in the whole fucking country does it. We don't. Not while I'm alive." He thumps his fist on the table again to emphasize his point.

I approach the table slowly, not wanting to be drawn into this debate. It's the same one Viktor has been pushing for months. He wants to expand the business into sex trafficking, but Ivan has refused at every turn. Though Ivan can be a mean old bastard when necessary, he has his morals, certain lines he refuses to cross, and no one and nothing changes his mind.

"Dimka!" Ivan says, his craggy face breaking into a smile. "Glad you could make it tonight! Maybe you can talk some sense into my numbskull son here. I'm getting too old for his constant bickering. Come. Sit. Let us talk of better things."

Viktor gives me a look of pure loathing. He's hated me for as long as I can remember, and that hatred has only grown over the years.

"I wouldn't want to bother you any longer with my bickering," he says stiffly, rising from the table. "If you'll excuse me."

I sit down across from Ivan, relaxing fractionally as the shadows settle over me.

"So," Ivan begins. "Josef tells me you found our thieving friend last night?"

"Freddy won't be a problem anymore," I confirm, taking a sip of the aged whiskey the waitress places on our table.

"That's good."

I shrug. "Maybe. But I think he was working with someone else."

"You think he was working on behalf of the Italians?" Ivan's eyes lose focus as he contemplates this. "He has been friendly with them in the past, it's true, but he's never been a problem before. He's even helped us on occasion. Why start working for them now?"

"I don't know. It might not be the Italians, though they'd be my first guess. But don't worry. I'll find whoever it was before I leave. Two weeks should be more than enough time to sniff them out."

Ivan looks more concerned about my last statement than the fact that there is an unknown enemy still as yet unaccounted for.

"Are you still set on leaving us, Dmitry?"

"We had a deal. We both agreed that I more than paid back the debt I owe."

"After all this time, I had thought our relationship had grown into something more than a debt to be paid."

I keep my expression carefully blank, not responding to the guilt pinching my gut. "Of course, Ivan. You know how much I respect you. You've been like a father to me. But it's time I move on. I have ambitions beyond being your Beast."

"I never liked that term," he says with a frown.

I shrug again. It's irrelevant. That's what everybody calls me, and I can't say the nicknamed is unearned. I've been his enforcer, and when the situation calls for it, his hit man, for over a decade. I've been a scarred beast for much longer than that.

"What will you do with all your free time?" he asks. "Ah, yes, your carvings, right?"

"Woodworking."

"Yes, yes. You are quite good, I'll give you that. But you know you'll never earn even a fraction of what I pay you making tables for the rest of your life."

"Money, I have," I say. "What I need is a job with less death and bloodshed."

"Pity," Ivan says with a sigh. "You are so good at it."

I know he's not talking about my skill carving wood. I'm a killer. A damn good one at that. But after so many years, the blood on my hands has started taking a toll, though I would never admit it out loud. I haven't gotten a good night's sleep in years. My dreams are plagued with images of the men I've killed, the widows and orphans I've left, the people I've ruined and hurt.

No, it's time for a change. But first I have one last despicable deed to do. One last act as Vasilek's Beast, before I can simply be Dmitry.

The change in the music alerts me that the auction is about to begin.

In two weeks, I'll be free. I can give this life up forever. But only after Daisy is mine.

Ivan notices my alert gaze and gives me a curious look. "Looking for some female companionship? About time." He chuckles. "I've been saying for years that what you need is a good lay. You are always so tense."

I ignore him, my gaze glued to the stage. The first few females brought out are completely uninteresting. You have your usual hard-eyed women who've been on the block more times than they can count. The ones addicted to smack or meth. They don't sell for much, usually just enough to get their next fix.

Then they bring out the first of the wide-eyed innocents. Girls who have gotten themselves into trouble and have no option except selling their virginity to pay their way out. Girls like my Daisy. Virgins sell for a premium and bring in the largest crowds. The first couple of innocents are thin and pale. Weak looking, watery-eyed girls seconds away from all-out hysterics. I wonder how Daisy will handle this as the bidding escalates. Will she break down and cry like these first two?

I hope not.

While this charade is necessary for me to take possession of her, I don't want to frighten her unduly. I'm not planning on using and discarding her the way these bastards will do to the poor girls on stage. No, I'm playing for keeps. If there was any other way to get Daisy into my possession, I would have taken it rather than subject her to these animals' greedy looks.

No, I don't want to scare her. The first time I fuck my beauty, I don't want her cowering in fear. Though it's probably more than I should hope for, I want her to want me back. I want her to be as mad with lust for me as I am for her. I won't touch her until she's begging for me, needy and wanting.

I shift uneasily in my chair, cock hardening at the thought.

Finally, the gavel comes down. The girl is sold to the lecherous old bastard in the front row. The girl on stage stares at the wizened old geezer and attempts a smile. She has no idea the sick perversion she's walking into. She probably thinks she dodged a bullet, being sold to an old man instead of one of the hulking, cruel-eyed men surrounding the stage like so many jackals circling a dying gazelle. Even though I only come to these auctions when Ivan insists on meeting here, even I've heard whispers about Lazeray, the old man up front. Just wait until he gets that poor girl alone. She won't be smiling anymore.

Finally, Daisy is led onto the stage. I'm so used to seeing her in her bright yellow waitress uniform that I don't recognize her for a moment. Though I've spied on her nearly every night for the past six months, I've never seen her wearing anything like the lacy white lingerie she has on now.

Her pale skin shines all the brighter in the smoky, dim atmosphere. Like an angel descended from heaven itself, trapped in the deepest, blackest pit of hell.

And I have no illusions about who dropped her into this hellhole. I've never claimed to be a good man. Some say I'm not a man at all. Just an animal. But I swear, once I get my hands on this perfect creature, she'll never want for anything ever again. I take care of what's mine. And she will be mine. I've spent a considerable amount of time and money to make sure of it.

She holds her head up, high and proud, so unlike the previous girls. That alone makes her stand out like a star in the black sky. Her blond hair catches the light as it cascades around her shoulders and down her back.

One look at her face and I know I was a fool to think she might break down in tears like the others. No, her face is the picture of pride and determination. Here she is, in the city's most depraved club—a veritable hell on earth—but her face is calm and relaxed, her gaze fixed on the wall over our heads as if she knows she's too good for any of us poor souls.

The bidding starts off even higher than the others. Though the last two were also virgins, Daisy's calm demeanor and enchanting beauty have captivated the crowd unlike any of the others.

The bidding escalates, steeper and quicker than I anticipated. Maybe allowing her up on the auction block wasn't the best idea after all...

I have made a fortune over the years, it's true, but much of that money is tied up in investments and bonds. My liquid cash is comfortable but limited. And it looks like I will have to spend a good chunk of it here tonight.

"Thirty thousand," I bid, earning a few looks.

On stage, Daisy's gaze jumps to mine, a strange look of relief crossing her face.

"Thirty-five," a smooth voice counters, drawing Daisy's gaze away from mine. Viktor smirks at me from the other side of the room, his eyes laughing.

Damn him. I should have known he'd place a bid the moment I did. In his mid-thirties, you'd think he'd be too old to harbor such a petty grudge, but a day doesn't pass in which he doesn't try to get one over on me. And now I've just handed him the perfect revenge. It would make his year if he bought the woman I wanted out from under me. And out of all the men in this room, Viktor is perhaps the only one who has pockets deeper than mine.

"Forty thousand," I say, raising the bid.

Viktor quickly counters. He won't give in, I know that. And my funds are limited, unlike his.

Ivan laughs, the sound a hollow memory of the deep laugh it used to be. The years are working against him.

"Just like brothers, you two. Always fighting about a new toy or girl."

"You want me to stay on longer?" I ask Ivan quickly, not able to keep the growl from my voice. "Then I want the girl."

Interest sparks in his eyes. He raises a hand, signaling the auctioneer over, all the while studying my set face. The room erupts into whispers as the crowd tries to figure out why the auction stopped.

"I'll give you the girl," he says. "If you continue working for me for another six months. Times are precarious right now. The Italians are planning on making a move against us very soon. I need you with us when they do."

Six more months. Fuck.

I was so close to getting out. Two weeks and I would have been done with all this shit. Two fucking weeks and I would have been on an island beach somewhere, making a living with my hands, nothing to worry about but my next woodworking project. But that picture is hollow without Daisy by my side.

"Fine," I agree, my eyes returning to Daisy. "Whatever it takes."

Chapter 4

DAISY

All eyes stare at me, lust filled gazes taking in my exposed body. Sizing me up, calculating how much they think I'm worth. I bite my lip to keep from trembling. I have to do this, I remind myself. There's no other way.

I resist the urge to adjust the little scrap of material that passes for underwear in this place. The bra and panties they forced me to wear are made of white lace so fine you can practically see through them. I keep my head up high, refusing to let these animals see the fear in my eyes. God, what kind of man come here to buy desperate virgins to sleep with?

I keep my gaze trained on the wall high above their heads, but in my periphery, I study the faces of the men, trying to envision spending one night in any of their beds, let alone a full week.

As I take in the patrons of Iniquity, the city's most notorious club, I have to swallow to keep the bile down. Though some of the men look well off—they'd have to be to afford the outrageous club fees—others look like they just stumbled in off the street; gangsters, drug dealers, pimps.

The girls who prepared me earlier and dressed me in this skimpy lingerie had a few tips for me, but I know nothing can prepare me for the reality of what I'm about to face.

The bidding begins all too quickly. I hold my breath, willing the price to rise higher and higher. If I can't make at least twenty-five grand here tonight, all this will have been for naught. I have to make enough to pay off Ray's debt, plus Iniquity's twenty percent cut from whatever bid I earn.

From somewhere in the shadows, a deep, masculine voice calls out, "Thirty thousand."

Relief nearly makes my limbs go weak. I did it. No matter what happens this week, at least I know I made enough money to save my family from the Russians.

My eyes strain to make out the hulking man in the shadows who made the bid. He's wearing a suit, sitting at the furthest end of the room, behind some sort of red-velvet roping. From this distance, all I can tell is that he's massive. That alone should terrify me. That, and the careful, no-contact distance everyone else seems to keep from him. Whoever this man is, one thing is certain: he's dangerous.

Before I can make him out properly, another bid rings out. Thirty-five thousand?! That kind of money will go a long way toward my college fund. I might even be able to start next semester.

When I turn to look for who made the bid, my heart stutters in my chest. The man is much smaller than the first. Objectively speaking, he's handsome, with a straight nose, dark hair smoothed neatly back, and a cleft in his chin. But the smile he tosses across the room is full of arrogance, and his eyes are hard and cold. I've seen men like him before; suave and good-looking, but with a cruel streak a mile wide. My mother's dated her fair share of this particular type of monster.

The big guy bids again. Forty thousand. Even though his size alone should scare me silly, I find myself hoping he wins the auction. The thought of the sly businessman with the cruel eyes taking my virginity makes my blood run cold.

The businessman counters again. "Forty five."

Then a much smaller figure next to the hulking shadow raises his hand. The auctioneer steps away from the podium and approaches the man. All bidding stops. Confusion ripples through the crowd. What's going on?

The cruel man's face hardens, eyes narrowing in anger.

After a long few moments, the auctioneer returns to the podium and bangs the gavel.

"Sold, for forty thousand!"

What just happened? Forty? I thought the bid was forty-five? Who bought me?

I don't have long to contemplate it before I'm whisked off stage so the next girl can take my place. Two stone-faced Russians flank me on either side while I wait to be claimed.

The crowd parts and the largest man I've ever seen slowly approaches. He's well over six feet tall, and so wide two of me could hide behind him. Probably three. He has short, dark hair, and is clearly well off if his expensive suit is any indication. He must have had the suit custom–made to fit his massive frame.

As he moves closer, I have to force myself not to react. On the right side of his face there's a huge, ugly gash starting at his temple and traveling all the way down to his chin. Though he's still too far away to tell clearly, I can see a few other dark lines crisscrossing the right side of his face, and a thinner scar on his left cheek. It's like someone took a knife to his face, carved him up, then sewed the flayed skin back together.

I'm so busy wondering where he could have gotten those scars from that I don't notice how close he's moved until suddenly I'm staring straight up into his startling green eyes. I want to look away from his fierce gaze, but I can't. I'm mesmerized by the sharp, almost feral intensity in it.

The man he was sitting with, the one who caused such a scene, has followed in his wake, but the pull of the big man is so strong I barely notice him until he's standing right in front of me. He's much older, thin and frail, leaning heavily on a cane.

Which one made the winning bid?

The thought of being taken by a man old enough to be my grandfather makes my stomach turn.

"She certainly is pretty, Dmitry," the older man says to the scarred one beside him, his gaze sharp despite his obvious years. "I just hope she's worth all the trouble." His lips quirk up in a smile.

My heart restarts at his words. Dmitry won the auction. I won't have to sleep with the old man.

Despite my fear, my stomach flutters at the way Dmitry stares at me. Like a blind man seeing light for the first time. I have no idea what captivates him so much, but I find myself staring back with just as much intensity. His possessive gaze travels down my body, searing my skin like a brand. I shiver.

Despite his scars, or maybe because of them, his face, his entire demeanor, captivates me. Scars or not, he's the most compelling man I've ever seen.

And the most frightening.

After what feels like an eternity, Dmitry breaks eye contact to answer the old man. "She is, Ivan," he says. My insides tremble at the rumble in his deep voice.

Then Dmitry's words click in my brain and my head whips to the side. Ivan? As in Ivan Vasilek? The head of the Russian syndicate? My mouth drops open.

My God...

I look back into Dmitry's emerald eyes, studying him more closely. Anyone who has dealings with Ivan must be bad news.

"What's wrong, Dmitry?" An acid voice cuts in, making me jump. "Couldn't fight your own battle? You had to run to my father?"

Dmitry's face pulls into a scowl, making the scar on his cheek stand out all the more. He shrugs out of his black suit jacket and wraps it around my shoulders before he turns his back to me, blocking me from the other man's view.

As I scramble into the jacket a wave of rich, masculine scent washes over me, calming me, making me feel safer than I have all night.

"She's mine, Viktor," Dmitry says, his voice low in warning.

"Yeah, for a week. We'll see what happens after that. Her family has a habit of getting themselves into trouble. She'll be up for auction again. I have no doubt she'll be in my bed eventually."

I suppress a shudder, unconsciously stepping closer to Dmitry. Warmth radiates from his pressed linen shirt, instantly making me feel calmer.

"Though after spending a week with The Beast," he continues, "she may not be quite so pretty."

The Beast? Is that what they call this man with the intense stare and frightening scars? What did I get myself into?

Ivan scowls at Viktor before offering me a small smile and a wink. "I'll see to you later, Dmitry. Enjoy your night."

Dmitry nods, then turns to me. "Come on, let's go." He places a hand on my back and guides me ahead of him out of the room.

"I'll see you soon, sweet Daisy," Viktor calls after us. Dmitry's hand presses harder against my back and I could swear I hear a growl come from him.

I don't glance at him again until we're outside in the parking lot. When the door closes behind us, he unknots the black tie at his throat and unbuttons his crisp white shirt.

Fear spikes through me. Is he planning on taking me here, in the parking lot?

But as soon as his shirt is off, he hands it to me.

"Put this on."

I hand him back his jacket and eagerly cover my bare flesh. The shirt is so big I have to roll the sleeves back several times to free my hands. Once it's buttoned, Dmitry turns and leads the way to his car.

The full moon overhead allows me to get a clear view of Dmitry's back, and I have to contain a gasp.

Like his face, there are long puckered scars slashing across the skin. Some of them run perfectly parallel to each other, others bisecting each other at various angles. The scars are purple, puckered, ugly lines, but underneath them, Dmitry is built like a brick house, his golden skin encasing bulging muscles.

He turns to open the car door for me, and his chest is just the same. Tribal tattoos cover his upper chest and shoulders, but underneath the ink, there are more scars covering his chest and stomach.

When he catches me staring at his chest, the skin around his eyes tightens, but other than that, his face remains alarmingly blank. I jerk my gaze down to the pavement at my feet.

He holds my door open and I climb into the expensive black sports car. If his extravagant bid wasn't proof enough of how rich he is, this car would certainly do the trick. It must be nice to have so much money you can waste on frivolous things like shiny new sports cars and virgin women at auction blocks.

I grit my teeth, determined to get this over with and get back to my life. I have to figure out a way to get my mom and brother away from Ray. If I don't, I know it's only a matter of time before he goes into debt again, just like Viktor predicted. I clench my teeth, remembering Viktor's threats about taking me into his own bed.

Over my dead body.

The ride to his house is uncomfortably quiet. I turn to look out the window, watching the night flash by. I'll sleep with Dmitry tonight. I'll let him do whatever he wants with me for the next week. But before the week is out, I'll come up with a plan to get us free from Ray, one way or another. I was sold for forty grand.

Even after paying off Ray's debt and giving Iniquity their cut, I'll still have nearly twelve thousand left—more than enough to get us out of Philadelphia.

We drive for a long time, leaving the city behind. After traveling through endless forests for nearly an hour, Dmitry finally pulls into a small gravel driveway that leads to a modest log cabin set back in the woods. It's completely isolated. If he turns out to be a sadistic son of a bitch, there's no one around to hear me scream.

I wrap my arms tight around my chest and I climb out of the car. Dmitry looks me up and down, his gaze sending sizzling awareness throughout my body. Then he motions with his head that I should follow him inside.

The interior is surprisingly light and airy. Pine floors and a minimal amount of furniture give it a sense of openness, but the comfortable looking couches and chairs make it feel safe and homey at the same time. It certainly doesn't look like the home of a serial killer, but then, Ray doesn't look like the type of man to sell his girlfriend's daughter in order to pay his debts. Looks can be deceiving.

Once inside, Dmitry turns to stare at me, the overhead lights illuminating his scarred body in stark relief.

Even though I've seen his bare chest outside Iniquity, it's still a shock, especially in this bright light. Under his expansive tattoos, the skin is puckered and raised in angry red slashes all up and down his torso. What happened to him? Who could have done something so grisly?

I meet his eyes with difficulty. His intense stare makes the hair on the back of my neck stand on end, my heart thudding loudly in my ears. This is it. Time to pay up. Time to honor my end of the bargain.

Chapter 5

DMITRY

She looks nervous as she steps into my house, stopping right inside the doorway. She probably expects me to pounce on her the moment we're inside. And damn if that image doesn't make my dick twitch. It's been painfully hard since I saw her up on that stage. But here, knowing I finally have her all to myself, knowing I can take her, fuck her like no other man has before, mark her as my own...

I can't believe she's a virgin. In the months since I've been watching her, I've never seen her with another man, so I assumed she was inexperienced, but I never imagined she was so completely untouched. To think that I will be the first man to touch her, to kneel between those creamy thighs and enter a place no other man has before...

I halt those thoughts before I lose my tenuous grip on control.

I won't hurt her. Won't take her against her will. I have a whole week. Plenty of time for her to settle in and rid herself of her fear of me. I have no idea how I'll convince her to stay past a week. I know she could never truly want me, but everyone has their price. I just need to find hers. And I can't frighten her on the first night or I'll drive her away for good. I need to go slow, show her that there's nothing to fear.

I stare at her, riveted, as she examines her surroundings. Her beauty calls to me unlike anything I've encountered in my long, dark life. She doesn't deserve to get taken by the likes of me.

Ever since my parents were killed and I was carved up like a roast turkey, the only women who have willingly fucked me are hard-eyed whores who charge triple what they normally would to touch a beast like me.

When I saw Daisy a few months ago, I couldn't help being drawn to her. Daisy. What an apt name. So pure and innocent, just like the delicate white flower she's named for.

As soon as I saw her, I knew she was mine. But as much as my dick is throbbing to drive home inside her, I have to keep it contained. For now.

Her wide eyes take in the room, the furniture, the shelves of books and small carvings, before finally coming to rest on me.

Her gaze travels down the scars marring my body. I resist the urge to turn away to hide them. Better she sees the type of monster I am now. Maybe her fear will keep me from taking her right here on the floor like an animal, the way my body is urging me to.

But when her gaze meets mine again, it's not fear I see in her eyes. Instead, there's curiosity, as if she's trying to figure out what caused the ugly marks. Then the curiosity fades, replaced by determination.

Before I can send her to her room for the night, she raises her chin defiantly, grips the hem of her shirt—my shirt—and pulls it up over her head.

My mouth goes dry as I take in the pale perfection of her skin, the graceful curves of her hips, the plump swell of breasts above the lacy white bra. My heart beats heavily against my rib cage. I want to roar in satisfaction at finally having her in my house.

I ball my hands into fists to keep from touching her creamy skin. I try to find my voice, to tell her she doesn't have to do this, not tonight, but my throat closes up, stopping me.

She steps towards me. I'm frozen to the spot, unable to move. My clenched fists tremble at my sides. I know I should stop her, but I'm fiercely curious to see what she plans to do.

She steps close, so close I can feel the heat coming off her skin. She's so small she has to arch her neck all the way back to look at me. She reaches one hand behind her back to undo her bra. The lace falls away, exposing her perfect tits.

My mouth waters, dying to tease those perky little nipples with my tongue, to suck those ample breasts into my mouth and make her squirm with pleasure.

She extends one slender hand and rests it on my chest. She doesn't even flinch away when her perfect skin brushes against the hideous scars.

Shit... I have to tell her to stop, tell her she doesn't have to do this. But... just one more minute. I need to see what she's going to do next. Maybe she'll beg me to let her go. Plead with me not to take her the way I so desperately want to.

But she doesn't do any of those things. In fact, the longer I stay still, the less nervous she becomes. She touches my chest with both hands now, confidently running them across my skin. I try not to flinch as she grazes the puckered, angry lines.

Her hands settle on my hips and she rises up on her tiptoes as high as she can. She seems frustrated by her small stature. Her mouth only reaches to my chin, the brush of her delicate lips against my jaw sends a jolt of heat straight to my dick.

She reaches up, cupping the back of my head with both her hands and tugs me down. I oblige her unspoken command and lower my head just enough for her to brush her lips against mine.

I try to stay still, but the sweet innocence of her kiss breaks my control. My mouth descends on hers, and I thrust my tongue into her sweet mouth, devouring her like a starving man. Despite my aggressive kiss, I somehow manage to keep the rest of my body still.

She seems surprised by the kiss, but doesn't pull away like I expect. Instead, she puts one hand on my chest to hold herself steady while she presses closer, giving me greater access.

Her kiss undoes me. My blood roars in my ears, flowing downward, causing my dick to swell to painful proportions. If I don't step away now, I'll have her pinned against the wall as I fuck into her tight virgin pussy.

I break away from her with a growl. Her sweet whimper of protest almost breaks my resolve. My whole body is throbbing. I desperately need to jerk off.

She stands there in that tiny scrap of underwear, staring up at me. I watch her tremble as she takes in my ruined visage. But she doesn't flinch away.

No, she holds my gaze, those pink, plump lips parting as she looks up at me with those innocent doe-eyes,

Fuck...

My hand lifts of its own accord, fingers skimming down her creamy white shoulder. I just need to feel the softness of her skin.

Just once, I promise myself. Just one caress and I'll send her off to her room like I'm supposed to. Anything more would fuck up my plans.

My hand caresses her tiny shoulder. Her skin is just as soft as I imagined. I let my fingertips linger, slowly sliding down her arm, soaking up the feel of that soft, perfect skin under my calloused fingers.

I mean to step away, but as I skim the soft curve of her hip, those pink, inviting lips part on a gasp, her eyes widening with some strong emotion.

I watch those eyes, waiting for the fear and revulsion to fill them as I touch her, but it never does.

I take a step closer, my chest practically brushing hers. My mind conjures up all sorts of filthy images. God, what would it feel like to pin her to the wall right here, to have those soft tits mashed up against my chest?

I allow my hand to linger on her hip, the heat of my palm sinking into the thin material separating her bare skin from mine. My gaze becomes fixed on those parted lips.

She still hasn't flinched away, hasn't tried to stop me in any way. I feel like I'm caught up in some spell, unable to tear my gaze away from hers, unable to step away like I know I should.

I lean down, closer and closer, until I'm just an inch away from those perfect lips. I can feel her breath on my face, those soft puffs of air against my lips. I can practically taste her.

A need so strong I feel like a man possessed takes over. I have to taste her again.

My lips press against hers, soft and sweet. I trace the seam of her lips with my tongue, needing to get inside her fucking body any way I can.

She makes the sweetest little moan when she opens for me and my tongue delves into those silky depths, licking and tasting, probing deeper and deeper, needing to explore every inch of that silky mouth.

Then it happens. She shifts against me, her soft tits pressing against my chest, and I just fucking lose it.

I push her back against the wall and attack her mouth, kissing her deeper, harder, unable to get enough.

I delve into her over and over again, barely letting her come up for air. My throbbing cock presses up against her stomach and I can't fucking stop myself from thrusting against her. She gasps at the feel of that hard ridge, but she still doesn't push me away.

I know that isn't an excuse for what comes next. I mean, this is what she thought she was here for, right? Sex? She doesn't know that she has a choice in this. She doesn't know she could have told me no.

When she makes that sexy little moan again, I pull back, needing to see those lust clouded eyes and pretty, parted lips swollen from my kiss.

Staring at her, a hunger overtakes me, a fucking animistic need to taste all of her, to fucking devour her.

I drop to my knees in front of her, my nose skimming the apex of her thighs, drinking in the musky aroma of her arousal.

Fuuucck...

I need to see. Need to feel if she's wet for me. Need to fucking taste her between these pretty pink lips down here. I can't stop myself.

My hands skim up her thighs, eyes locked on her face above me, still waiting for her to stop me. But she doesn't

She just stares down at me, her eyes wide, those beautiful lips still parted as she watches. And she lets a fucking beast like me caress those creamy white thighs, lets me pull her panties down her legs, and stare at fucking nirvana between her thighs.

She clean-shaven, every inch of her bared to my gaze. My mouth salivates, heart pounding out of my chest. I meet her gaze again, still waiting for her to protest, to cringe in revulsion at letting an animal like me near a perfect creature like her.

My eyes are drawn back to her glistening pussy. I lick my lips, mouth watering at the sexy musk.

She's wet for me.

Just one taste, I promise myself. Just one fucking taste and I'll leave her alone. When will I ever get this chance again? Just one fucking taste...

I lick up her slit, tongue delving into her slick folds.

Fuck...

I groan deep in my chest. God, she tastes fucking amazing. Like honey and cream. I can't stop myself from taking one more taste, my tongue probing even deeper, seeking out that hot, wet core and drinking in her juices.

I'll never get enough of this; it's fucking heaven.

Her pussy lips are smooth and plump, glistening with my saliva, just begging for my mouth again.

I'm going to pull back. Really, I am. But then she does something that makes it impossible. She shifts, parting her legs, opening her thighs wider to give me better access.

I pounce. Like an animal with the scent of prey, I attack her, shoving my face in between her thighs. The taste of her explodes on my tongue.

And she moans.

She fucking *moans*.

I drag my tongue through her silky folds, lapping at her like a wild fucking animal, completely out of control.

She gasps, her hands coming down to grab my head. But she doesn't push my face away. Oh no. She pulls me harder against her, her fingers tangling in my hair.

She squirms and writhes against my face, caught between my hard body and the wall behind her. Sexy little whimpers work their way free, driving me to the brink of sanity.

With my tongue, I find her hidden nub and press down. She jerks against me, her grip in my hair tightening painfully.

I continue to apply pressure to her clit until she's bucking against me, wild and completely uninhibited. Then I suck it into my mouth, hard.

She comes on a scream, her whole body clenching and jerking. I continue lapping at her, drinking in her juices until the last shudders pass.

With more control than I thought I possessed, I rise to my feet. Her head is resting back against the wall so I have a perfect view of her flushed face and rosy lips, her eyes still closed in ecstasy. She's never been more beautiful.

Unable to help myself, I reach up and run my thumb along her plump lower lip.

Her eyes flutter open, still glazed and hazy with the force of her orgasm.

My dick twitches. I force myself to step away from her before I push her any further tonight.

"Your room is the second door on the right," I bite out before snatching her panties off the floor and fleeing down the hall.

I strip out of my clothes the moment the door is shut and jump into the shower. My body's on fire, cock so hard my head is already slick with precum.

Under the hot sprays of water, I wrap my fist around it and squeeze, imagining it's her fist wrapped around my cock, or better yet, her lips. I picture her on her knees in front of me, her warm, wet mouth wrapped around my shaft, tongue swirling around my head while she sucks at me.

Imagining those wide, innocent eyes of hers looking up into mine, my orgasm crashes through me. Hot cum lashes the shower wall, her name a shout on my lips.

Chapter 6

DAISY

I lean back against the wall, my body shivering with pleasure after the most incredible orgasm of my life. Then Dmitry steps away and practically runs down the hall to get away from me.

What the hell?

Embarrassment floods me. What did I do wrong? I know he was aroused; I saw the bulge in his pants. I thought he was attracted to me. Why would he run away?

I shake my head, too dazed to try to figure him out.

I've never been with a man before, not like that. There have been a few clumsy fumblings in high school, groping in the dark, but I've never had a man's face pressed between my thighs like that, his tongue probing my most secret places. And I've never come so hard my eyes rolled up into my skull like that.

I pick Dmitry's shirt up off the floor and head into the room he indicated as mine. Slipping his shirt back over my naked body, his warm scent surrounds me, making me feel safe, which just goes to show how badly that orgasm addled my brain. I've never been less safe in my life.

I've always been good at reading people, but I can't seem to get a feel for Dmitry. He's obviously powerful, with his massive body and corded muscles. Dangerous.

How did he get those scars? And what exactly is his connection to Ivan and the Russian Mafia?

Yes, he's most certainly dangerous. And probably a criminal to boot.

But if he's so bad, why didn't he have sex with me just now? I practically threw myself at him, determined to get it over with. But instead of taking what I offered, he chose to give me the most excruciating pleasure of my life, while taking none for himself.

Why didn't he sleep with me? I know he wanted to. It was there in his eyes: lust, need, and a strange kind of yearning. I don't understand what went wrong.

Pushing it from my mind, I explore the small room. It's clean and neat, with a bed, a small chest of drawers, and an end table with a reading lamp.

Seeing the dresser, I realize I left my suitcase with all my clothes at Iniquity. Dmitry was in such a rush to leave, I completely forgot about it.

Damn. What am I supposed to wear all week? I couldn't even find my panties on the floor though I'm sure I tossed them on the floor nearby. Maybe he'll let me go home for a few changes of clothes tomorrow.

I hug Dmitry's shirt closer to me, breathing in his scent as I contemplate my predicament. At least I got a reprieve for tonight. A small victory. I won't have to worry about him taking me until tomorrow. Who knows, maybe I'll get lucky and he'll continue to run from me all week. For some reason, that thought makes me feel worse.

I stretch out in the soft bed. The evening's events have exhausted me more than I thought possible. Tomorrow there will be time enough to worry about everything.

I yawn, lethargy overtaking my muscles. Hugging Dmitry's shirt tighter around myself, I sigh and drift off to sleep.

The next time I open my eyes, the room is filled with sunlight.

I jerk upright, momentarily forgetting where I am. Yesterday's events flood back to me, especially the scene in the living room last night.

My cheeks heat as I remember the incredible feeling of his tongue exploring my most private area. Then an image of him fleeing away rises up, and my cheeks burn for a different reason. Did I do something wrong? Is that why he ran away?

I stumble to the bathroom across the hall and brush my teeth with the toothbrush I find there before wandering out of the room in search of Dmitry.

I find him in the kitchen, spatula in hand.

His eyes rake down my body before he turns his back on me.

"Want some breakfast?" he asks in that gruff voice of his.

My eyes are drawn to the play of strong muscles under his crisp white collared shirt. Like yesterday, he's dressed in a suit, another narrow black tie knotted perfectly at his throat. His jacket hangs on the back of one of the kitchen chairs. The cut of the linen shirt only emphasizes how large his chest is, the impressive breadth of his shoulders. I remember how, underneath that shirt, his golden skin hugs all those lovely muscles. My mouth goes dry, heart racing in my chest.

I clench my jaw, annoyed at myself. I shouldn't be feeling this way about him. He bought me, for God's sake. What kind of man does that? Not the kind I should be attracted to, that's for sure. This is a job. Nothing more.

He turns to face me, his expression carefully blank.

"Sit down. You like eggs?"

"Um, sure." I'm thrown off balance by his kindness, so at odds with his appearance.

I take a seat at one of the wooden chairs and he places a plate of eggs and bacon in front of me. It feels strange to be served. I'm usually the one cooking and serving, both at home and at work. I can't remember the last time someone cooked for me.

We eat in silence. He keeps his gaze mostly on his food, but every once in a while I catch him staring at me, as if he can't help himself. Feeling more than a little awkward, I rack my brain, searching for something to talk about.

"This is really good," I say after my first few bites, pasting a bright smile to my face. Masking my anxiety and engaging people in idle chit-chat is my specialty. Useful talents for someone working in the service industry. No matter how rude or obnoxious my customers are, I can always hide my emotions behind a smile and some polite banter.

"You sound surprised," he responds, glancing at me with those intense green eyes.

"A little. I've never known a man who could actually cook before. My brother wouldn't know how to boil an egg if his life depended on it." I smile, thinking of Jeremy.

"Well, when you live alone, your choices are learn to cook or starve."

"True. Maybe one day Jeremy will grow up and learn to take care of himself," I say with a light laugh.

Chapter 7

DMITRY

I stare at her, transfixed by her soft laughter, the seemingly easy way she can sit here across from a monster and make conversation.

I can't stop my gaze from dipping down to her body. She's still wearing my rumpled shirt. It's so big it swallows her whole, the front gaping open to reveal the tops of her breasts. I like the way she looks in my clothes. It shows she's mine. Only mine.

Once I have her here for good, she'll wear nothing but my clothes. Or nothing at all...

I slide my hand into my pocket, my fingers finding the lacy scrap of panties she wore last night. My dick grows hard remembering what she let me do to her. And even after I attacked her like an animal, she can sit so calmly across from me and make polite conversation. My Daisy isn't as delicate as she appears.

For the first time since I began planning this, I begin to think I really might have a chance at convincing her to stay. Somehow, against all odds, she doesn't seem afraid of me.

Not yet, at least. And for a man accustomed to being feared by the most ruthless criminals in the city, the fact that Daisy doesn't cringe away every time I look at her is a small miracle.

But behind her smiles and meaningless chatter, I can still sense her unease. I'm an expert at spotting it; I see it often enough, from friend and foe alike. And I can see it in her eyes right now. The way she won't meet my gaze for more than a few seconds at a time, the way her eyes are constantly darting around the small kitchen, how her fingers keep plucking at the hem of her shirt.

She's definitely nervous, even though she's putting on a good front.

No, I can't fuck her yet, but damn if I know how I'll keep my hands off her. I want to bury myself inside her. Claim her. Make her mine.

She continues chattering away, talking about Jeremy and her mom. It's obvious she loves them, even if she does sound exasperated at times. I notice she doesn't mention Ray. There's no love lost there. From what I know of the bastard, he's a drunk and a user. He also dabbles a bit in gambling. This isn't the first time he's owed us money, but thanks to Josef's efforts on my behalf, it is the most money he's owed us by far.

I sit in rapt attention, listening to her chatter on about everything and anything. There's something soothing about listening to her clear, light voice; hearing about her life, her family, her dreams. I want to know more about her. I need to.

But the longer she talks, the more uncomfortable she seems to get, meeting my eyes briefly, before her gaze flits away to bounce around the kitchen once again.

It's then that I notice I haven't said a word in almost ten minutes. I'm not used to talking to anyone for more than a short conversation, just long enough to relay any pertinent information about a job.

Wanting to put her at ease, I seize on the last thing she said, something about hoping to start college in the fall.

"What do you want to study?"

She blinks at me, her face coloring slightly.

"Art," she says, a bit shyly. "I've taken some classes in high school, and the city library sometimes has a free class every now and then, but it's hard to find any advanced courses outside of a university."

"Art?" I act like this is new information even though I've spent the last six months watching her draw. "What kind of art?"

"Painting, mostly. But I also love to sketch, and I've done a bit of sculpture in the past; I'd be interested in taking some classes in that, too. "

I know she loves to draw, but in all the months I've watched her, I've never seen her paint before. Why not?

Her interest in sculpture also surprises me. I wonder what she'd make of my carvings. Part of me hungers to share that with her, to give her a glimpse of something so personal, something I haven't shared with anyone before. But a larger part of me is terrified of opening so much of myself to her.

She's only here because you paid her to be, I remind myself. *Don't read any more into it than that. Once her week is paid, she'll be gone before you can say 'beast'.*

Unless I can figure out her price.

"So," she asks when the silence stretches out between us. "What do you have planned for today?" As soon as she says that she blushes to her hairline, as if remembering why she's here.

"I have to work," I say, standing to carry the plates to the sink. And I have an errand to run; our conversation gave me an idea.

"Oh." She looks surprised. She probably expected me to spend all day ravishing her. And after the amount of money I spent on her, the fact that I'm not taking advantage of every minute is monumentally stupid. But I need to get this Freddy business taken care of, and she isn't ready for me anyway. Maybe a day alone will help settle her nerves.

"Make yourself at home while I'm gone. There's a computer in the living room, along with some books to keep you occupied. The fridge and the pantry are fully stocked. Help yourself to whatever you want. If you need anything else, I wrote my cell number over there," I say, motioning to the whiteboard hanging on the kitchen wall. "Just text me what you need and I'll pick it up. I might not be back until late."

With that, I grab my jacket and hurry out the door before I can change my mind.

Chapter 8

DAISY

He ran away. Again.

I stare at his retreating back as he hurries out of the house, locking the door behind him.

What is going on? Why would he spend forty grand just to go down on me and cook me breakfast? It doesn't make any sense. This guy must be out of his mind.

Oh, well. Looks like I get another reprieve. After washing the breakfast dishes, I wander around his house, unsure what to do with myself.

The first thing I notice is that there aren't any pictures on the wall. No photos or personal items anywhere, in fact. The bookshelf around the fireplace is huge and expertly crafted. I run my hand along the intricate carvings etched along the sides. The light wood shines in the early morning sunlight. It's beautiful.

Something on the shelf catches my eye. It's a carving of an owl, small, but exquisite in detail. There are several more carvings scattered about on the shelves, some of animals, others of people. One of the females looks eerily similar to me. How odd.

They're beautiful, all of them. I wonder where he got them from.

I turn the statue of the female over, looking for any indication of who the artist might be, but there isn't any type of identifying mark. Huh. I wonder... Did Dmitry make this himself? Maybe there's more to him than meets the eye.

I absently toy with the sculpture while mulling over the puzzle that is Dmitry. He buys me for an exorbitant price at a sex auction, but doesn't actually have sex with me; he has some kind of connection to the Russian mob, but lives out here in the forest, away from the glitz and glimmer of the city; he is richer than anyone I've ever met, but keeps a simple house full of hand-carved knick-knacks; he appears forbidding and intimidating as hell, but he's shown me nothing but kindness and respect since the moment he pulled me off that stage.

That man is full of contradictions.

I pace around the house, disturbed by the small part of me that is actually looking forward to staying here with him and unlocking the puzzle of who he is. The part that is intrigued by the man behind his scars and size and frightening demeanor. The part that is excited to explore this explosive chemistry between us— eager for more of what he gave me a taste of last night.

Is this how my mom feels every time she enters into a new relationship with another lowlife? My stomach tightens at the thought. I've always been disgusted by the way she could fall for men so obviously screwed up, and here I am, excited by the prospect of hopping into bed with a bona fide criminal.

I have no illusions about how bad he is. He's in league with the freaking Russian Mafia. I shouldn't be having any thoughts about him other than a desire to get as far away as possible.

But there's a difference between my situation and my mom's, I remind myself. My mom chose those men and dragged us into debt and trouble time and time again. I don't have a choice in this matter. If I don't do it, my family will die. I'm doing what I must to keep them safe. And if I happen to enjoy it just a little—well, it's better than being traumatized by the experience the way I would be if someone like Viktor had bought me.

There's no way in hell I'd be able to tolerate that man's touch. Under his handsome appearance is a snake. A predator. I've seen it enough in mom's more charming boyfriends. A memory flits through my mind—one of those charming snakes creeping into my room late at night...

With a sharp shake of my head, I banish the memory. Dwelling on the past doesn't do any good. I need to focus on the present.

I continue exploring Dmitry's house, attempting to redirect my thoughts. He keeps his home immaculate. Everything neat and organized, so different from my own house. I do my best to keep it clean, but it's difficult when I'm the only one who ever cooks or cleans, on top of working forty hours a week at the restaurant.

Sometimes it feels like an impossible task, especially since Ray and Jeremy are such pigs. Even my mom doesn't seem to mind the mess all around the house. I'm the only one who cares if we're living in filth, so all the cleaning falls to me.

I wonder if my mom and brother even realize I'm gone yet. Would Ray have told them about the auction? Probably not. He wouldn't want to admit to my mom how far in debt he really was.

I call my house from Dmitry's landline, since I left my cell and everything else in my bag at Iniquity. My mom answers on the third ring.

"Hey mom, I wasn't sure if you'd be working today."

"I have the late shift tonight. Ray told me you got a job out of town for the week. Something about taking care of an elderly woman?"

Taking care of the elderly? Well, I guess I have to give him points for creativity. As a cover, it isn't half bad.

"Yeah, it's just for the week. The money was too good to pass up."

"Good. We need it. We're late on the rent again."

"Don't worry, this job will cover it," I say, thinking about the twelve grand I'll have left over when everything is said and done. "Hey, did Jeremy leave for his job interview yet? That was today, right?"

"Oh, that," she says. "Well, he talked to me about it this morning. Apparently, they weren't offering as much money as he thought, so he decided to skip the interview and try to find something else."

"Are you kidding?" I ask, appalled. "Mom, this is the first interview he's had in *months*. You just said how we need the money. I can't believe you let him ditch it!"

"And you just said the rent is covered, so we're not in trouble just yet."

I bite the inside of my cheek to keep back a scream. "But you didn't know I had the rent covered until just now," I say slowly, holding onto my patience by a thread. "How could you let him skip the interview when you didn't think we could even afford to keep a roof over our heads for another month?"

"What do you expect me to do, Daisy?" she says, exasperated. "I can't force him to take a job he doesn't want. He didn't want to bus tables for other people. You know how he is. He has pride."

"Pride won't put dinner on the table. He needs to pull his weight," I say, anger creeping into my voice.

"He will; he just needs to grow up a little. His heart is in the right place. He'll find something eventually."

Yet I'm forced to sell my body to pay off her boyfriend's gambling debts? Resentment coils deep in my gut.

Sometimes I wonder why I bother trying to keep her and my brother afloat. I make enough at my waitressing job to afford a small apartment on my own if I wanted. The only reason I stay at home and put up with Ray and all the bullshit is because I know she wouldn't be able to afford the rent and utilities without my paycheck. The fact that she sees no problem letting Jeremy skip through life without any responsibilities or consequences irks me to my core.

"Yeah. Sure. Look, I have to go. I have cleaning to do." I hang up, too angry to even say goodbye.

Even if I were to find a way to convince my mom to leave Ray, do I really want to be solely responsible for her and Jeremy? But if I don't get them away from him, it's only a matter of time before Ray runs into trouble with the Russians again. I can't risk that.

Frustrated, I search the computer desk in the living room for some paper and a pencil. The first drawer is locked, but the other two hold a small collection of graphite sketching pencils, my favorite brand too. What a funny coincidence.

The feel of the pencil in my hand already has my muscles relaxing. Drawing always helps to calm me when life seems to be spinning out of control.

I idly sketch, letting my mind wander, pouring my emotions out on the page. Some people keep a journal of written remembrances, but I prefer to keep a sketch journal. Drawing the important moments of my past week allows me to more effectively capture the emotions of the moment.

I sketch a scene from the night before, when Ray grabbed me in my bedroom. The fear and adrenaline from that instantly swamp me, making it difficult to breathe.

I push through the remembered fear, focusing instead on the feeling of strength and power that rushed through me when I shoved Ray off of me. I try not to remember the resulting crash, the destruction on my sketches and most valued possessions. I stay focused instead on the pride and exhilaration I felt knowing I was able to fight him off, knowing that I was able to defend myself against him instead of letting him push me around.

Keeping that feeling of self-sufficiency within me to ward off the fear and helplessness, I begin sketching another picture, of one of the girls on stage at Iniquity, her limpid brown eyes swimming with tears as an old man with a lecherous smile steps forward to claim her.

Next, I draw Dmitry the first time I saw him, half in shadow, half in light, his eyes narrowed dangerously as the rowdy crowd parts in front of him like the Red Sea.

By the time I feel in control again, I've sketched a dozen scenes from the previous night. The last one, an image of Dmitry on his knees in front of me, his blazing eyes staring up from between my legs, has me shifting uncomfortably in my seat.

God, the feel of his wicked tongue licking and suckling at me…

I stand abruptly, heat pooling in my abdomen unbidden. I need some fresh air.

I wander into the backyard, struck by how pretty it is out here in the woods. Living in the city as I do, I've never spent much time in nature. I realize I don't even know where it is I'm staying. It's outside the city, obviously, but I was too distracted last night to pay attention to where he was driving.

There's a large detached garage at the edge of the forest. Curious, I try the door. Locked. Huh.

I walk around it, trying to peer into the windows, but they are all covered with closed blinds, making it impossible to see inside. What could he be hiding in there?

The answer is obvious. I shake my head. He must be running drugs for the Mafia. Of course. Why else would he be involved with them?

He's a criminal, I remind myself. He probably keeps their product stashed out here, in the middle of nowhere. I can't imagine it's easy to store this stuff in the city, what with the scores of police and drug-sniffing dogs.

My stomach clenches uncomfortably. He's just another low-life drug dealer, like most of my mom's boyfriends.

I head inside, more restless than I was before. I wander aimlessly around the house again, not used to having so much free time on my hands. I decide to take a shower to wash off the stink of Iniquity from last night.

His bathroom is just as clean as the rest of the house, but I'm surprised to find the shower fully stocked with female beauty products. He even has my favorite shampoo, conditioner and body wash. Why does he have all this? How often does he frequent these sorts of auctions?

The thought of him routinely buying women and screwing them turns my stomach.

Once I've showered, I realize I don't have any clothes to change into. I forgot to ask Dmitry to pick up my bag from the club before he left.

With a shrug, I rummage through Dmitry's drawers until I find another white button up shirt to wear. It's huge on me, just like the last, but once I roll up the sleeves a couple times and find a belt to cinch it around my waist, it's manageable.

When that's done, I head to the kitchen to start on dinner. He wasn't kidding when he said the fridge was stocked.

I lose myself in the familiar task of getting dinner ready, but as the sun slowly sinks behind the trees, my thoughts turn toward what tonight will bring.

He'll probably expect to have sex tonight. I can't imagine he'll wait another night before claiming what he's paid for. Come to think of it, giving me a day to adjust before pouncing on me might have been his plan all along. Based on the contents of his bathroom, he's probably practiced in the art of coaxing shy virgins into bed. I wonder how many he's had before me.

My mood sinks, and I forcibly turn my mind away from such thoughts.

When it's fully dark out and he still isn't home, I carefully clean up the kitchen, putting aside a plate of stir-fry for him to have when he gets in. Then I find something to read from the bookshelf and settle on the couch to take my mind off my unpleasant thoughts.

Chapter 9

DMITRY

I spend a fruitless day chasing down all my contacts with links to the Italians, but no one is able to give me any info on Freddy's potential partner. Finally, out of ideas, I park myself outside a restaurant known to be frequented by Nicholas, the Italian boss. Maybe I'll get lucky and find a new informant.

I fiddle with the lace thongs still in my pocket as I wait, the sun getting hotter and stronger as the day wears on.

I wonder what she's doing now? Just knowing that she'll be in my house, waiting for me when I get home has my heart beating a little faster, my balls drawing up a little tighter.

I think back to last night after she'd fallen asleep in the spare room. How I stood there in the doorway, watching her sleep, the pale moonlight spilling through the window to caress her golden hair and creamy skin.

I stood there for what felt like hours, my cock throbbing even after jerking off in the shower, debating whether I should wake her up and take her then and there. After all, I did pay for her. She knew what she was getting into.

I held myself back, but just barely. When she entered the kitchen this morning, sleepy and rumpled and oh, so fuckable, my chest squeezed. The shy, sexy smile she gave me reassured me I did the right thing by waiting.

But fuck… I don't know how much longer I can hold out.

The door to the restaurant opens, bringing me back to the task at hand.

Shit! Who just went in there? I have no idea.

What the fuck is wrong with me? I'm supposed to be staking out the joint and instead I'm daydreaming about a girl. Fuck.

I run my hands down my face, willing myself to get my head in the game. I don't daydream. I don't fucking lose focus. I've had her for less than a day and this chick is already fucking with my head. I need to fuck her already. Maybe then I can get my head out of my ass.

It's late by the time I finally concede defeat and head home. My stakeout achieved nothing except to frustrate me even further. I've wasted the entire day on a wild goose chase with nothing to show for it. That's one whole day of my time with Daisy, time that could've been put to better use getting Daisy accustomed to me, calming her fears so I can finally get between her thighs.

At least I accomplished one thing on that front, I think as I glance at the bag on the passenger seat. I was lucky to find a craft store open this late. I try to picture her face when she sees what I got her. Maybe if I buy her enough gifts, her gratitude will compel her to stay.

I suppress a snort.

It would have to be a fuck-load of expensive presents, I think sourly.

I'm surprised to find a light on in the living room when I return to the cabin. And there on the couch is my Daisy, fast asleep with a book on her chest, her golden hair spread around her like a halo.

She's wearing another one of my shirts and, despite my shitty day, I smile. My chest immediately feels lighter just seeing her here in my house. In my clothes.

I place my package on the kitchen counter and I pick her up gently. Her body is soft and warm, and so much smaller than my own. I cradled her close and carry her to my bed. I can't help myself. I need her near me.

Contentment wells up seeing her in my bed, where she belongs. Seeing her there calms the beast inside me in a way nothing else over the years ever has.

Mine.

Even if I haven't yet figured out how to keep her longer than a week. I still have time. She wants to go to college, right? Maybe I'll offer to pay for her classes. Maybe she'll agree to stay then. It all depends on how badly she wants to go.

Contemplating this new idea, I head to the kitchen to grab a quick bite. There, on the top shelf of the fridge, is a plate carefully wrapped in plastic wrap, just waiting for me.

She made me dinner? A queer sensation fills my chest. No one has made me dinner in, fuck, I can't even remember. I'm sure my mom cooked once in a while when I was a boy, but nothing I can remember. It was too long ago.

Why would she do this? I all but abducted her and forced her into my bed to serve my depraved desires. Why would she go through the trouble of cooking me dinner?

Of course, she has no idea just how much I am to blame for her current circumstances. If she ever found out...

But she won't. Only Josef knows and I trust him more than I do anyone else.

I sit down at my computer to research a few potential leads while slowly savoring the stir-fry. It's delicious, even cold.

I move to place the plate on the desk but freeze when I see the pile of detailed pictures there. I pick up the first one and frown in dismay. The level of detail is impressive in such a small sketch, but the image of Ray gripping her arms has my blood boiling.

When I orchestrated the plan to bankrupt Ray, I didn't count on him physically harming Daisy; he was only supposed to convince her to go to the auction. None of my research into him revealed him to be the violent type. But if he harmed her in any way, even God himself won't be able to save him from me.

The next picture only sends my mood plummeting further. My own scarred face glowers up at me. Every ugly slash laid out with exquisite skill and accuracy. The shading only lends to the sinister feel of the sketch—half in shadow, half in stark light.

With a sinking feeling, I flip through the pages, stopping at the last sketch in the pile. My heart stutters in my chest at the close-up view of my face as I lap between her legs. Like the other picture, the scar on my face is depicted in excruciating detail, but in this one, there's no sinister feel to it; only dark delight. My eyes glint teasingly up from the paper, my lips curling into a wicked smile.

Is this what I looked like to her that night? Not like the animal I imagined.

I rub a hand against the strange feeling expanding in my chest.

I shut down the computer, thoughts of hunting for leads forgotten.

Right now, Daisy is sleeping soundly in my bed. There's time enough for work tomorrow.

When I climb into bed beside her, the mattress dips, causing her to roll right up against my bare chest.

My cock throbs, instantly hard. It's been too long since I've fucked a woman. Years. I stare at the delicate skin of her neck, my gaze following it down into the dark recess of the button-up shirt she's still wearing.

Fuck… Maybe I should wake her up. Just fuck her and get it over with. She won't protest; she knows why she's here. It's what I paid for, after all.

But then she sighs and snuggles closer, resting her cheek on my chest.

That strange sensation from earlier comes back, stronger than before. What the fuck is wrong with me? I'm going soft; that's what.

Ignoring my aching cock, I wrap my arms around her and pull her closer. Burying my face into the crook of her neck, I breathe in her soft, feminine scent. I lay there long into the night, just holding her and listening to her soft breaths.

Chapter 10

DAISY

I wake up slowly, unwilling to leave this hazy, warm contentment. But when my eyes flutter open, the warmth doesn't dissipate. If anything, my body heat ratchets up another notch when I realize I'm in Dmitry's bed, my cheek pressed against his bare chest.

How did I get here? The last thing I remember is lying down on the sofa to read. He must've carried me in after I fell asleep.

A flash of remembered sensation flits across my mind; strong arms holding me close, his lips pressing into my hair, just grazing my neck.

I smile to myself. I thought it was just a dream.

I peak up at Dmitry, checking to see if he's awake yet. His eyes are still closed, his breath slow and even.

I've never woken up next to a man before. It's surprisingly pleasant. Even if he is a criminal.

I know I shouldn't be feeling anything towards him. I mean, he bought me at a sex auction for God's sake. But even knowing this, I still can't keep a smile off my face.

With Dmitry asleep, it affords me the perfect opportunity to study him without those penetrating eyes of his boring into mine.

My gaze first traces the dark tattoos inked into his golden skin. The tribal design is beautiful and exotic, and just a bit wild. It suits him. I wonder if he got it done to hide the puckered scars on his chest.

This close to him, I can make out every angry slash. There are a lot more than I originally thought. Where could he have gotten these from? I glance up to the deep furrow bisecting his face. My fingers itch to trace it, but I don't want to risk waking him up.

Funny, but even though it's only been a couple of days, I'm already getting used to his appearance. The sight of his scars doesn't frighten me nearly as much as it did when I first saw him.

I allow my gaze to travel down his strong chest, to where the blanket rides low on his hips.

He's naked under the covers. My whole body flushes, imagining what he looks like under the covers. Glancing up once more to make sure he's still asleep, I slowly lift the edge of the blanket.

I feel myself getting damp as my eyes follow that bronzed skin all the way to the V of his hips. Then lower. I catch only a glimpse of something thick and hard and undeniably male, when the back of my neck prickles with awareness.

Heat rushes to my cheeks and I drop the blanket. I look up into deep, slightly sleepy green eyes.

Thankfully, he looks more confused than anything else, his normally sharp gaze still drowsy.

"I slept all night?" he asks, his voice rough with sleep. "I haven't slept a full night in…" he trails off, eyeing me strangely.

Uncomfortable under that gaze, especially after getting caught checking him out while he slept, I leap up, his shirt clutched protectively around me.

"I'll go make breakfast," I say too brightly.

I busy myself in the kitchen, manically whipping eggs and frying bacon, as if I can bury my embarrassment under a mountain of breakfast food.

He's a criminal, I chastise myself. *He's involved with the mob. You CANNOT have feelings for someone like him.* Hell, I barely even know him. The thought of having feelings for him is ridiculous. But ever since that first night, when he lavished me with pleasure beyond my wildest dreams, my traitorous body has been hungry for more.

It's just a defense mechanism, I reason with myself. My mind knows I have no choice but to give him my virginity, so it's making my body more receptive to him, to mitigate any fear or pain I might experience. That sounds logical enough. That must be what this is.

But what the hell is he waiting for already? He bought me for sex, but it's been two days now and he hasn't touched me since that first night. Why is he waiting so long?

Then a horrible thought enters my head. Maybe he's disappointed with me. Maybe, after that first night, he decided I wasn't worth the amount of money he spent. Maybe I'm not pretty enough or sexy enough. Humiliation blooms in my stomach.

I shake my head, trying to push the embarrassment away. I shouldn't care what he thinks. It doesn't matter if he finds me attractive or not. I'm here for one reason: to clear my family's debts.

But what if he plans on getting a refund for me?

Back at Iniquity, the girls told me stories about men returning girls to the auction. They warned me not to fight the man who buys me. They said it's easier for everyone if I just submit to whatever he wants me to do, or else he could end up returning me for a refund. Then, not only would I lose whatever money I would have earned from the auction, but I would still have to pay Iniquity the twenty-percent auction fee—which means I'll be in even more debt than I was to begin with.

And if Dmitry does return me, will Viktor then take me for himself like he threatened?

The blood drains from my face. No, I can't let that happen. I won't let that vile man touch me. Dmitry can't return me. At least, if he does, he won't return me as a virgin. I won't let him. One way or another, Dmitry is going to get what he paid for.

Maybe he's been waiting for me to make the first move. That could explain why he hasn't touched me since that first night. But I'm completely inexperienced. I wouldn't even know where to begin.

Then Dmitry walks into the kitchen wearing a white t-shirt and a pair of black sweatpants slung low on his hips. His eyes rake over me.

"Smells good," he says in that gruff voice of his.

I try to remember what the girls at Iniquity told me about men. About what they like.

With his gaze still on me, I step up to him and grasp the waistband of his pants.

Surprise crosses his face, then his gaze dips back down to where my shirt gapes open at the front. Lust glitters in his eyes.

It's that look in his eyes that gives me the confidence to fall to my knees in front of him. Looking up at his towering figure, I lick my lips, trying to imagine what he might taste like. I've never done anything like this before, but the girls at the auction explained the basics.

Gathering my courage, I slide his sweatpants down, revealing his thick shaft inch by inch. When it's fully exposed, I just stare in awe. It's massive. I mean, with a body like his, I assumed he'd be big, but it's so far beyond my imagination. I feel a moment of hesitation. Will I even be able to get my mouth around it?

As if sensing my hesitation, he tries to step back, mumbling something about me not needing to do this, but I latch onto his bulging thighs, not letting him step away from me.

"You don't have to do this if you don't want," he says again, but his gaze stays locked on my lips, eyes slightly glazed as if he's picturing what I'd look like with his cock between them.

Letting his expression feed my courage, I lean in, inhaling the scent of warm male. I reach one hand up to lightly grip his shaft, mesmerized by the silky skin over the steel core of his member.

I lick my lips again, glancing up. His mouth is slightly open, eyes transfixed on my face as if he can't quite believe what I'm doing. Experimentally, I lick the wide, purple head, marveling at the smooth feel of him. A bead of moisture appears on the tip.

Gaining courage, I lap at it. It's salty, yet sweet. He lets out a groan that goes straight to my core.

The look of awe on his face is a heady, powerful thing. I meet his rapt gaze, then, very deliberately, I run the tip of my tongue from the base of his shaft, all the way up to the tip, swirling my tongue along the ridge of his head.

More salty-sweetness explodes on my tongue and I let out a low moan.

Dmitry is staring, slack-jawed, slightly panting. He wants this. He *really* wants this. All thoughts of Viktor and the auction flee my mind. All that's left is a desire to make him feel as good as he made me feel that first night. I may be inexperienced at this, but if my mouth on him feels half as good as his tongue did on me, then there's no way I can screw this up, even if I'm not quite sure what I'm doing.

I open my lips and oh, so slowly, wrap them around his head, running my tongue along every inch of the sensitive tip.

Another groan escapes him and he grabs the edge of the counter behind him for support.

He's so big my lips feel stretched to the max. I take a deep breath in through my nose, then slowly slide his cock further inside. I'm not even halfway down before his head prods the back of my throat. I swallow reflexively and he sucks in a breath, a look of pure ecstasy on his face.

I do it again, feeling my throat muscles squeeze his head. He groans, loud and deep, his head falling back. I begin moving up and down on his shaft, swallowing every time he reaches the back of my throat.

Between the feel of his slick cock in my mouth and the satisfied groans coming from above, my core clenches tight, as if begging to be filled.

It feels so wrong to be turned on by this. I was bought as his sex slave; I shouldn't want him like this. I shouldn't be enjoying this. It's fucked up. But I can't help it. I've never done anything like this before, and knowing how much he's enjoying it makes me feel sexy; powerful in a way I've never felt before.

I suck on him, running my tongue all along his shaft. I feel myself getting wetter and wetter with every groan that rumbles in his chest.

Without warning, he grabs my shoulders and yanks me up to a standing position. Before I can protest, he's lifting me off the ground and laying me out on the kitchen table. The breakfast plates crash to the ground, forgotten. He grips the edges of my shirt, and with one swift jerk, he rips it open. Buttons fly and cool air caresses my skin.

Laid out before him, completely naked, legs spread wide open, I feel like some sacrificial virgin about to be devoured by a beast.

And devour me he does. I don't even have time to blink before his head is between my legs, his hot mouth covering me. He eats at me like an animal, tongue wildly lasing through my folds, thrusting inside me, then pressing hard against my clit. His mouth is everywhere, lips, teeth, and tongue all working together, the sensations too overwhelming for me to separate them out.

"Your pussy tastes so fucking good," he growls out between licks. "Like heaven. I could eat you forever."

Whimpers rise up my throat. His dirty words should embarrass me, but instead, they turn me on all the more.

When he draws my clit between his lips and sucks, I completely lose it, bucking wildly. I had no idea sex could feel like this, so strong, so overwhelming. Just when I think I can't take anymore, Dmitry slips a finger inside my eager core.

"Fuck. You're tight," he growls. "So fucking tight. And all mine." He goes back to devouring my pussy while he thrusts his finger inside me. Despite my tightness, he slips another finger inside. I'm so wet I can feel my juices running down between my ass cheeks, onto the table beneath me.

"Please," I whimper, thrusting my hips in time to his fingers, unable to take the intense pleasure coursing through me. Pressure builds up, spiraling higher and higher. I thrash wildly under his assault, not sure how much more I can take.

"Please, what? What do you want, baby? You want more of this?" he asks, sucking my clit into his mouth while thrusting inside me again.

"Oh God, yes!" I cry out, bucking again and grinding my pussy into his face like a wanton slut. "Please, oh God! Please, Dmitry!"

"Please what? What do you want? I want to hear you say it, Daisy. I want to hear you beg for my cock."

His words send fire racing along my skin, making me burn even hotter. "Please, Dmitry," I beg. "I want you inside me. I have to feel you inside me."

Dmitry leans over me, his fingers still lodged deep inside my channel.

"You want me to fuck you?" he asks, emerald eyes fierce as he stares into mine. "You want me to fuck into your tight little virgin pussy?"

I bite my lip, writhing on his fingers, begging with my body. God, it's so wrong to be this turned on. My head thrashes back and forth, body on the brink of what I know will be the most incredible orgasm of my life, but just as the pressure reaches the brink, he begins removing his fingers. My walls clench around him, trying to keep him inside, but its' no use. I whimper at the aching emptiness.

"Please, Dmitry? God, I need you..." I writhe, excited to the point of pain. I need his hands on me, his mouth, his teeth, his tongue...

I reach out and start yanking his shirt up and over his head, needing to feel his skin against mine. He freezes but doesn't stop me. As soon as it's gone, I wrap my arms around him, bringing his bare chest flush against mine. We both moan at the contact. I shamelessly thrust my hips against his until I feel his hard cock sliding between my pussy lips. My juices coat him as I slide myself up and down his length.

"Fuck," he grunts out, eyes squeezed shut as I rub myself against him like a cat in heat. "You are so fucking wet. You need me inside you, baby? You need me to fuck you?"

"Yes. Please, Dmitry…"

"If I fuck you, you'll be mine. Do you understand? No one else will have you, ever. You are mine."

"Yes, yours. Yes. Please!" I cry out, barely knowing what I'm agreeing to. All I know is I need to feel him inside me, stretching me, filling that aching emptiness.

He grins, triumphant. Despite the need coursing through my body, I feel my chest squeeze at the sight of his smile. It's the first time I've seen it, and it transforms him from merely compelling to nearly beautiful.

I stare up at him, transfixed, while he lowers himself onto me. His head slips through my slick folds and he positions himself at my entrance. Without taking his eyes from mine, he thrusts forward with one swift stroke.

I feel a pinch of pain, there and gone. I groan in relief as my over-sensitized nerve endings get what they're begging for. He starts fucking into me, rough and wild, giving me just what my body's craving.

I arch up into him, reveling in the slick, hard feeling of him sliding in and out, the rough friction of his chest against my nipples, the hard slap of his hips against mine.

Dmitry grips my hair in one of his hands, yanking it back and forcing my mouth up to meet his. The tang of my arousal on his lips is so naughty, so hot. His mouth slants over mine, his tongue thrusting possessively into my mouth as he takes my body, claiming it, possessing it.

Pleasure sings through my veins, so intense I turn and bite down on his shoulder, my teeth sinking into hard muscle.

He groans, low and deep, the sound sending shock waves racing along my nerve endings, straight to my clit.

I explode, all my muscles locking tight. Wave after wave of pleasure crash through me. I cling tight to Dmitry's hard body, my safe harbor during the storm.

My walls clench tightly around him, milking him until his own orgasm explodes from him. Hot jets of fluid pump inside me, marking me like a brand.

He collapses on top of me, chest heaving. I relish the crushing weight of his body over mine, my mind still hazy, body warm and languid.

When he catches his breath, he slowly eases out of me. I feel a warm gush of fluids leak out between my ass cheeks and blush at the mess we must be making of the table.

He stands up and looks down at me, spread eagle on his kitchen table, his cream still dripping from my exposed sex.

I try not to shiver at the possessive glint in his eye. This man has been where no one else ever has been before. He's made my body feel things no one else ever has.

Despite the circumstances that brought me here, I can't help but feel extraordinarily grateful that Dmitry was my first. He's made this experience so much more incredible than I ever thought it could be. Brought me more pleasure than I ever could have imagined.

And he still has me for another five days. Assuming, of course, that he chooses to keep me...

DMITRY

I look at my angel, spread wide after I just fucked her. After I took her virginity the way no other man ever will. She was so sweet, so innocent, yet she responded like a wild cat in my arms.

Yesterday, when I held her late into the night until finally falling into a blissfully nightmare-free sleep—the best night's sleep I've had in years—I had resigned myself to waiting. I promised myself I wouldn't touch her, that I'd keep my distance no matter how badly I wanted her body wrapped around mine. But for some reason, this morning she sought me out and willingly fell to her knees to take me into that glorious mouth of hers. Why would she do that? Don't I scare her? Don't my hideous, ruined looks repulse her?

I've paid for my fair share of prostitutes years ago, and not one of them has come apart in my arms the way Daisy did just now. It's a trial for them to even pretend to enjoy themselves when they're with me, despite the ridiculously high fees I paid. Those whores couldn't get away from me fast enough.

But not Daisy. She wasn't acting for my benefit. Even now, she's still high from the incredible orgasm I gave her.

The feel of her pussy locking tight around me while she came... That feeling will stay with me the rest of my days.

And knowing that I was her first, the only man to ever touch her, and I brought her such pleasure that she was crying out my name, begging me to fuck her...

I feel my spent cock already stirring again as my eyes travel over her luscious body. What would it be like to have her here like this all the time, to be able to come home to her and take her willing body whenever I want?

My cum glistens between her legs and I suddenly wonder if she's on birth control. I'm sure she is. Who would auction themselves off for a week of sex with a complete stranger without taking the necessary precautions? But a part of my brain can't help but imagine my seed filling her up, making her body grow and swell with my child.

If I knock her up, then I could make sure she'd never leave me. I could keep her locked up here, ready and waiting for me all the time, filling this house with our children...

I blink the fantasy away. She wouldn't agree to stay here, to bear the offspring of a monster. Not until I find something enticing enough to convince her.

But first, I have work to do. Ivan scheduled a meeting for today, and if I don't leave soon, I'll be late.

I finally step back, tearing my eyes away from her beautiful body. I head to my room to dress, knowing I won't be able to keep myself from taking her again if I stare at her much longer.

"I have to go out," I say once I finish. "There's something I have to take care of. I'll be back later. Oh," I add, almost as an afterthought. "And I picked you up something yesterday. It's in the bag on the counter." I turn to leave.

"Wait, where are you going?"

Before I'm even out of the kitchen, she's on my heels, her delicate hands grasping my forearm.

"You're not going to Viktor for a refund, are you?"

"What are you talking about?"

She blushes and gazes down at the floor. "Some of the girls at Iniquity said that if a man isn't satisfied with her, they can return them for a refund. But you're not going to do that, right? I mean, I know it was my first time, but it was ok, right? You were…satisfied? You're not going to return me?"

My stomach plummets, blood turning to ice in my veins. Of course. She didn't want me. She just needed to get paid. Sucking me and fucking me was just a job to her. She's no different than any other whore I've been with; she's just a better actress.

Joke's on her though, because I meant what I said before I took her virginity. No other man will ever have her. She doesn't want me? Too fucking bad. I've tasted nirvana, and I'm never giving it up.

All I need to do is find her price. All whores have one.

"Oh, you're not going back to Viktor," I say, my voice low and dangerous. "I paid for you. You're mine."

Chapter 11

DAISY

He storms out, every line of his body rigid with fury.

I stand there, frozen, until I hear his car pull away. My stomach knots thinking about the expression on his face when I mentioned Viktor. Is that what made him so angry? There's clearly no love lost there, but I don't get why just the mention of his name would set Dmitry off like that.

At least he isn't sending me back to him though. A shiver runs through me as I remember the possessive glint in his eye when he said I was his. It should scare me silly, but instead, a warm feeling fills my chest, confusing me even more.

Sighing, I walk back to the kitchen to find what he left on the counter for me. Maybe he finally got me some clothes. It'll be nice to dress in something a little less resembling a tent.

When I open the bag, my jaw drops open. Inside is a veritable rainbow of acrylic paints. What is this?

I take them out, one by one. Underneath them all, there's a variety of different sized brushes and a book of thick-stock paper. Leaning against the counter is a folded easel, like the one Ray destroyed. He has everything here I need to paint.

My eyes turn misty. I love painting, but I can rarely afford the acrylics. He went out and bought this for me? Why? I don't understand. Yesterday morning I made a passing comment about my interest in painting, and that very same day he goes out and buys me a whole plethora of supplies to work with. Why would he do something like that for some girl he just happened to pick up at an auction?

I blink back the stinging in my eyes. I'm not used to getting gifts. Anything I want, I have to save up the money and purchase myself. Living paycheck to paycheck like my family does, we aren't big on presents. The last gift I received was a teddy bear Jeremy won me at a carnival for my ninth birthday. I still have that bear on my dresser at home.

Dmitry can't have known how much this would mean to me. Clearly rich, money probably means nothing to him.

But still, why would he go through the trouble of spending it on me? And on something so thoughtful, so personal.

A smile breaks across my face and I eagerly set the easel up near the computer desk where it gets the most light. I start off by sketching a picture of him from this morning, the low-riding blanket showing off his sculpted chest and ripped abs, his face relaxed and peaceful in sleep. Then another image forms in my mind: Dmitry leaning over me while I was spread out on the breakfast table, his breathtaking smile when I begged him to take me, when I agreed to be his. That smile that made my heart squeeze in my chest, made my insides turn liquid and melt at the sight.

Choosing this sketch to work from, I set it up on my new easel and prepare to paint.

Chapter 12

DMITRY

She's mine, whether she wants to be or not. I will find a way to make her stay.

I contemplate my options on the way to Iniquity where the meeting is being held. She wants to take art classes; I could offer to pay for her college. But then again, with the money she made off my bid, she'll be more than able to afford that on her own.

What else can I offer her? Jewelry? Trips to Paris or Rome or Barcelona? She doesn't seem like the type to be tempted by anything so superficial.

I pull up to the club just on time, but still no closer to figuring out what Daisy would want.

Iniquity has two levels: the basement, where Viktor holds his auctions once a week, and the strip club on the main floor. It's too early in the day for the strip club to be in full swing, but there are a few regulars there when I walk through the doors.

Raven, one of the regular girls, tells me, "They're set up back there."

I nod to her and head for the back where there's a small seating area reserved for the meeting.

I try not to curl my lip at the sight of Viktor getting sucked off by one of the stage girls. It's not as if I haven't seen worse here, but does he really have to do this here, now, when we're all assembling for a meeting?

Ivan's not here yet or I'm sure he'd have something to say to his wayward son. And if the looks of the other guys around are any indication, I'm not the only one put off by the display.

"Like what you see, Beast?" Viktor smirks at me as he shoves the girl's head down. I hear her sputter and gag. "If you're nice, maybe I'll let you watch while Daisy sucks my cock next week."

The thought of Daisy taking him into her sweet, warm mouth the way she did me this morning nearly sends me into a killing rage. My fists shake with the effort to keep from wrapping them around his skinny little neck and squeezing. I can almost see the way his eyes would bulge, the blood vessels popping as I constrict his airway. I can imagine the satisfying crack his bone would make as I snap his neck with one jerk of my hand.

"You'll never get your fucking hands on her," I growl. "She's mine."

Viktor grins wider, pleased to have gotten a reaction from me. "For another few days. But come Friday, she'll be opening those creamy white thighs of hers to me. Just think how grateful she'll be to finally get fucked by a real man, instead of some deformed animal like you."

Rage is a living, burning inferno deep in my gut, fighting to get free. My lips pull back in a snarl.

Over my dead body will this fucker even *look* at Daisy again, let alone get close enough to touch her. I'll tear him apart piece by piece before I let that happen.

Viktor grips the girl's hair in his fist and comes down her throat with a small groan. When he's finished, he shoves her off him and tucks himself back inside his pants, smirking at me the whole time, as if he wants me to see exactly what he plans to do with my girl.

The only thing stopping me from going for his throat is the two bodyguards next to him, watching me warily, their hands a breath away from their weapons. They'd pull their guns on me the second I went for Viktor. I might be able to snap his neck before they shot me; I might not. But with Daisy waiting at home for me, it's not a risk I'm willing to take.

"I told you it was only a matter of time before that family racked up another debt. Lucky for me, she's such a dutiful daughter that she's willing to work off her family's debt on her back. But don't worry, I won't make the mistake of sending her back to the block. No, we'll work out a deal privately. I'm sure she'll be more than willing to be my whore for as long as I want if I offer to clear her family."

My mind latches onto this piece of information. Some of my rage abates while I try to puzzle out what debt he could possibly be talking about.

"I already cleared Ray's debt. He doesn't owe us anything more."

"Not Ray," he says with a grin. "Her brother. He took out a loan two days ago. Seems to think he'll be able to pay it off by the weekend." He laughs mockingly.

"Jeremy borrowed money from you?"

"Runs in the family, I guess. Stupid fuckers will never learn. Lucky for me, though, don't you think?"

His barb doesn't faze me this time. I'm too busy figuring out how to work this to my advantage. Viktor may have just given me the leverage I need to keep her. Stupid fucker, indeed.

"How much does he owe?"

"Fifty large. More than Daisy made from you last week, if that's what you're thinking. And I already told you, she isn't going up for auction, so you can't buy her for another week."

"Wasn't planning on buying her from the auction again," I tell him truthfully.

"Is that your new car out front, Viktor?" Josef asks, pulling his attention away from me. "The black Ferrari?"

Viktor smiles arrogantly. "Sure is. Just picked her up yesterday."

"Damn, that must have cost a fortune. What is that? A V8?"

"V12," Viktor says. They begin talking specs, so I tune them out, instead hatching a plan to use Jeremy's debt to my advantage.

Fifty thousand dollars. What the fuck was her brother thinking. Kid can't even keep a fucking job longer than two weeks, and he's borrowing that sum from Ivan? He's either dumber than I thought or he has a death wish. I can't allow her irresponsible family to keep putting her in danger like this. Once I've completed my final six months for Ivan, I'm taking Daisy and getting her the fuck away from her idiotic family. I'll have to pull some of my stocks and bonds out earlier than I anticipated to pay this off, but no matter. This situation is exactly what I needed. Daisy will be mine.

Permanently.

Ivan finally arrives, putting an end to the conversation.

Ivan goes through the regular reports on various aspects of the business. When he gets to the Italians, I fill him in on the progress of my hunt for Freddy's partner, or lack of progress as it is.

"So if you can't find any leads, what makes you think there even is a partner? Seems like you're just wasting time with this wild goose chase," Viktor drawls from his lounging position on the couch.

I'm too used to this sort of baiting to let it get to me. The fact that he was able to get under my skin so easily with his comments about Daisy is both surprising and disturbing. I'm always in control. Always.

"We only recovered half the money," I say. "The rest was conspicuously missing."

"Maybe he spent it."

"He spent precisely half the amount of money that he stole from us? That would be quite a coincidence."

"But possible," Ivan says.

"Yes," I answer. "It's possible. But not likely."

"Is that your only piece of evidence?" Viktor taunts. "Some of the money is missing? Did he say anything when you interrogated him? Do you have any other concrete reason to justify wasting our time on this bullshit?"

I clench my jaw, but answer calmly. "He didn't last very long in the interrogation. And no, I have no other evidence that someone else was involved. But even you have to admit that Freddy wasn't the sharpest knife in the block. He couldn't have pulled off a heist like that on his own."

"Fine," Ivan says, cutting off whatever retort Viktor was about to say. "Keep on it for another couple days. If nothing pans out by then, we'll have to assume he was working alone."

I nod and step back into the background while the rest of them finish talking shop. When Ivan finally calls an end to the meeting, I hang back, waiting for Viktor to leave before approaching Ivan.

"Ah, Dmitry. How is your latest acquisition working out?"

"She's actually what I wanted to talk to you about. I heard her brother has accumulated some debt with us now."

"It's true," he says, leaning back into his chair. "That family just doesn't seem to learn. Poor girl is going to have a hell of a time if she intends to bail them out every time they run up a tab."

"I'd like to pay the family's debt," I say, cutting to the chase. I've never been one for idle chitchat. "And I'd ask that we stop lending them money. Any of them."

He studies me intently, his gaze still sharp despite the deep grooves age has carved into his once youthful face. He seems to age faster every time I see him. Though Ivan insists he's fine whenever I broach the subject, worry for his health tightens my chest. And the weaker he grows, the more bold the Italians will become. Viktor isn't strong enough to keep them in check. I can only hope I'll be out of this business for good by the time Viktor takes over. I have no desire to get caught up in the kind of bloodbath that will ensue when the Italians make their move to take over our territory as I know they will.

"Dimka, are you in love with this girl?" Ivan asks, his eyes snapping with delight.

Love? I blink. Of course I'm not in love with her. That would be monumentally stupid. I enjoy fucking her, sure. And keeping her locked up in my house to use whenever I want feeds a possessive streak in me.

The fact that she's the only woman I've met that doesn't cower in fear or flinch away in revulsion when she touches me doesn't hurt.

And yes, there's something intriguing about her willingness to sacrifice herself in order to save her family.

But love? I scoff. "Of course not. I'm just not finished with her yet."

Half his mouth quirks up in a smile. "Ah, of course. That must be it."

Ignoring his quip, I set about negotiating the absolution of her brother's debt.

"You are like a son to me, Dmitry. You know that, right? If you were to ask, I'd let this debt go without demanding any payment from you."

"Yes, I know. Instead of cash, you'd ask me to stay on working for you indefinitely, right?"

He grins. "Of course. As I said, you're family. This is a family business. Sometimes I think you are more like me than my own flesh and blood. If you chose to stay, you wouldn't be an enforcer forever. I'd give you more responsibility. More money, too. You'd be able to give this woman of yours anything she desires. Lord knows it's time I started delegating more. These old bones won't be around forever. Viktor tries, but you and I both know that once I'm gone, he won't be able to keep the Italians at bay for long. Not without your help."

"I appreciate the offer, Ivan. And I am grateful for all you've done for me over the years, but I have other plans. Other ambitions. I'll do what I can in the time I have left to weaken the Italians for you. But it's time I move on."

He's about to argue further, so I give him the one reason he won't be able to refute. "Besides, even if I did agree, you know Viktor would never stand for me to be in a position of power once he takes over. It's better for everyone if I leave before that happens." *Before Viktor has me killed,* is the unspoken message.

Ivan makes a face. "Alright, then. Alright. Six more months and you'll be free to do as you choose. But something needs to be done about the Italians. They're growing too bold. It's only a matter of time before they make a move. I can feel it. They'll strike soon."

His phone rings, interrupting the conversation. "Is that so," he says into the receiver, his gaze flicking up to mine. "No, no, you were right to call. I'm sending Dmitry over now."

"Well, Dmitry," he says, turning to me. "It seems your skills are needed elsewhere. One of Josef's bookies was caught skimming off the top. If it gets out that our own people think they can steal from us with impunity, we could be looking at a war sooner than anticipated. We can't allow that to happen. He needs to be made an example of."

Chapter 13

DAISY

I spend the day painting, taking occasional breaks to cook and clean up the house a bit—not that there's much to clean—he's surprisingly neat, an unusual trait for a male in my experience. But I feel guilty if I'm not doing *something* useful. It's strange to have all this free time on my hands. I'm so used to rushing around, between taking care of my family and the house, and rushing off to work, I actually find myself feeling guilty sitting and painting for so long.

Plus, even though I get annoyed with my family for never helping out, I do actually enjoy cooking and taking care of other people. I've been doing it for as long as I can remember. And right now, without the stress of waiting tables all day and no one making demands on me, the simple act of preparing a delicious meal and tidying up the house is actually relaxing, especially because I know he doesn't require it.

Cooking and cleaning are automatic to me, something I don't have to think about. It leaves my mind plenty of time to wander, and today my thoughts keep returning to this morning's mind-blowing events. It plays on a loop in my mind, over and over again. The feel of his rough, calloused hands on my skin, his hard body pressed up against mine, moving against me, inside of me...

When Ray first mentioned auctioning my body off, I was horrified. Never in my wildest imagination did I ever expect I'd actually *enjoy* being taken by the man who purchased me.

But the sex this morning was amazing. Incredible. And most astonishing of all, it was entirely my choice. He didn't force me into anything, even though he could have. Hell, it's the sole reason he bought me to begin with. But still, he left the choice up to me, never once pressured me into it.

I find myself humming as I cook dinner, eagerly waiting for Dmitry to come home. But as the sun begins setting, I begin to doubt he'll be coming home any time soon.

Sighing, I wrap up his dinner and put it in the fridge for later, then sit at my easel once again to continue working.

DMITRY

I stand outside the cabin in the fading light. A muscle twitches in my neck, a sure sign that I'm not yet calm enough to go in. I should have stayed away longer, but I couldn't help myself. I wanted to see Daisy. But not like this. Not until I'm in control again.

God, I hate it when they beg. The man knew what he was doing when he stole that money. He knew who he was crossing, yet he chose to do it anyway. The least the fucker could have done was take the consequences like a man. Instead, he begged and wept like a fucking child.

It's always worse when they beg.

Not because I feel pity for them; no, just the opposite. It's fucking disgraceful. Pathetic. It reminds me of my old man. He was a mean bastard when he was drunk, which was pretty much all the time. Around me and my mom and my little sister, he'd act tough—as if beating up on women and children made him a man or something—but whenever his bookies would come around to collect the money he pissed away on alcohol, he'd beg and cry and plead like the pathetic shitbag he was.

The guy tonight was just like that. He thought he was a big fucking man, getting one over on the Russian mafia, but when we came to collect, he broke down like the pussy he was.

And I still have another six months of this shit. Fuck.

Scrubbing my hands over my face, I try to get my shit together. Daisy is in there waiting for me. I need to lock it the fuck down.

Squaring my shoulders, I walk in to find Daisy sitting at her easel, lost in her art.

She looks so serene, so peaceful, sitting there in the last rays of the fading sun, her hand poised delicately over the canvas, a little crease between her brows as she scrutinizes her work.

She glances up then, surprise crossing her face as she notices me here. She was so engrossed in her work she didn't even hear the front door open.

For the first time, watching her paint doesn't calm me. Instead, all I can think is what would have happened if it wasn't me who walked through that door. It could have been any one of my enemies—and I have a lot—who came in here, and Daisy wouldn't have stood a chance.

Just like that fucker didn't stand a chance against me tonight. My mind flashes back to earlier, only instead of that man, it's Daisy I see on her knees, sobbing and pleading, begging me not to kill her.

Disgust surges through me, black and bitter. I'm a fucking monster.

Fuck. I can't stay here with her. Not after what I did. I don't deserve to breathe the same air as someone like Daisy.

Daisy's beautiful, shy smile transforms to one of confusion as I turn on my heel and head out the back door.

Chapter 14

DAISY

I'm so absorbed in my painting I don't even hear him come home. One moment I'm debating whether I've captured the right heart-melting expression on his face while he was sleeping so peacefully this morning and trying to sort out my conflicted emotions for him, and the next I glance up and there he is in the flesh, leaning against the door jamb in the kitchen. But his expression now is miles from the one staring up at me from the canvas.

I open my mouth to ask him what's wrong, but he turns away suddenly and storms out the back door.

What the...

I know he was angry this morning when I asked him if he was going to return me, but I just assumed that had to do with his own issues with Viktor. Based on their interaction that night, it doesn't take a genius to know those two despise each other.

But that doesn't explain his odd behavior now. Seeing him now, doubt churns in my stomach. Maybe he really was going to return me before I seduced him, and now he's regretting sleeping with me?

But then I remember his awe-struck expression when I went down on him, the almost reverent way he touched me, the look of pure triumph on his face when he finally took my virginity.

No, I can't believe that he regrets this morning.

I go to the back window and watch as he heads straight for the shed. He unlocks it with a key and pulls the doors shut behind him.

What the hell?

I knew it, I scold myself. I *knew* better than to let myself feel something for a low life criminal.

He's probably in there getting high. Fucking junkies.

What an idiot I am, to develop feelings for the first man to ever pay me any attention, the first man to touch me and make love to me. No, not make love. The first man to fuck me. That's all it was.

My God, I'm just like my mom… A man shows me a little attention and I fall all over him, despite knowing that he's a criminal, that he has ties to the Russian Mob.

I become more and more worked up, until I can't take it anymore. He may have bought me for the week, but if he thinks he's going to come in here high out of his mind and demand sex from me, he has another thing coming.

I storm out the back door, determined to give him a piece of my mind. If he wants to shoot up, he can damn well stay out in the shed until he sobers up.

I shove at the shed door, surprised when it actually gives way. I thought for sure he would have locked it. But when I open my mouth to deliver my angry tirade, the words die on my tongue.

He's…sawing?

I glance around in confusion. The entire interior is packed full of table saws, hand tools, and various sizes and colors of wood.

This isn't a drug warehouse. It's a...workshop?

I glance at Dmitry, still trying to fit this new information into my current mental image of him.

He stands there, shirtless and sweaty, a carving tool still gripped in his hand. He looks too shocked to say anything.

After a few moments, I blush. "Sorry, I thought you were...uh..." I hesitate, at a loss for words.

"You thought I was what?"

"I thought maybe you were getting high..."

His brows pull together, stretching his scar tight. "You think I'm a druggy?"

I blush even harder. "I didn't know what to think. This place is locked down like Fort Knox, and when you came home you didn't say anything, just took off for this place so..."

"And so you assumed I was doing drugs?"

I cross my arms defensively. "In my experience, when a man gets pissed and goes off alone, he's usually headed out to score some smack. It wasn't a completely unreasonable assumption."

His gaze stays locked on mine, but the angry set to his mouth softens a bit. "Ray?"

I shrug. "And a long line of boyfriends before him. How my mom keeps falling for dead-beat drug addicts is a mystery to me. You'd think she'd learn her lesson after the first one."

He doesn't say anything, for which I'm grateful. Talking about my mom's boyfriends always puts me in a foul mood. I'd rather not talk about them. Instead, I slowly take in my surroundings, noticing even more of those small wooden carvings that he had on his bookshelf.

"What is all this?" I ask.

"My workshop."

When it appears that that's all he's going to offer, I raise my eyebrows expectantly. He takes the hint.

"I had a shitty day at work. Woodworking helps me calm down."

I smile at this very human answer. "When I'm upset I sketch."

"I saw your sketches," he confesses.

"You did? When?"

"Last night. You left them out on the desk."

"Oh. I must have forgotten about them." I glance away, embarrassed. Most of those were of him. I wonder what he thought of them.

As if reading my mind he says, "They're good. Seriously impressive."

"Yeah?"

"Yeah. You have a gift."

I smile shyly at his praise. Then I look around the enclosed space again. There are not just sculptures in here, there's furniture too. Ornate tables and handcrafted bookshelves, all exquisitely done.

"So do you," I say, wandering over to a table in the corner with a larger sculpture on it. Standing about a foot tall, it's the head of some kind of animal, so masterfully done you'd almost think it was about to come to life. Its mouth is open, fangs fully on display, but it's the eyes that really grab your attention and won't let go. There's so much anger in them, and so much pain. How did he manage to capture such powerful emotions in a dead piece of wood?

"This one is beautiful," I say, running my hands along its spiky mane.

"It's just a beast. A ruined animal."

Something in his voice makes me peer more closely at the animal. Then I notice the deep groove carved into the side of his face, almost in the exact position as Dmitry's scar.

I look up at him, startled. Is he talking about himself?

My gaze travels to the scar on the side of his face. He turns away, hiding it from my view.

Without thinking, I reach out and cup his cheek, turning his face back toward me. I don't know what possesses me to do it, but I can't stand to think he's trying to hide his scars out of shame or embarrassment.

My fingers explore the rough contours of the jagged slash. His jaw tightens, but he doesn't stop me. For a moment his green eyes open wide, a look of vulnerability flashing in them. Then they shutter closed and he pulls his face away from my hand. He steps back, putting some distance between us.

Gathering my courage, I step closer. "How did you get the scars?"

He keeps his eyes averted, busying himself with cleaning up his tools. He's silent for so long I assume he isn't going to answer. Then, when he puts the last tool away, he says quietly, "It happened when I was very young."

"How young?"

"Nine," he says, leaning his big frame against the wall behind him.

I watch him for a moment, noticing the stiff set of his shoulders, the tension in his jaw. I close the gap between us, leaning against the wall next to him, my right arm pressed up against his left. The heat from his bare skin penetrates the thin cotton of the t-shirt I'm wearing. His shirt, again, since I still haven't asked about picking my bag up from Iniquity.

He stays perfectly still. I'm not even sure he's breathing. After a few moments, the stiff set to his muscles relaxes fractionally.

"What happened?"

I don't expect him to answer, but to my shock, he does.

"My dad was a drunk and a user. Not unlike Ray. He liked to beat up on me, my mom, and my little sister when he came home late at night. But even as a kid, I was big. Eventually, I was big enough to fight back. Nothing pissed the old man off more than me standing up to him. I still got my ass kicked. I wasn't strong enough to actually win against him. But at least he'd exhaust himself with me and leave my mom and sister alone."

He pauses, as if lost in that childhood nightmare. It's the most I've heard him speak since I've been here. I want to hear more. I want him to open up to me.

"So your dad gave you the scars?" I encourage when he doesn't continue.

"No. Not exactly." He shakes his head, coming back to himself. "I was planning on getting my mom and sister out of there. I had taken a job in a restaurant washing dishes after school. Under the tables, of course. I was saving up to get us all a bus ticket to Chicago, where my mom's sister lived. But my dad, he liked to gamble. Was always borrowing more money than he could pay back. And one day, before I could get them away from the bastard, some men came to collect. My dad couldn't pay."

"So they hurt you because of your dad's debt?" I'm unable to keep the shock from my voice.

"You sold your virginity to the highest bidder to pay off your family's debt, didn't you?"

Heat floods my face. He makes me sound no better than a whore. And I guess I'm not. And worse still, I not only sold my body for sex, but I enjoyed it. Even now, standing so close to the man who bought me, my body is responding. Heat is flooding my core, excited tingles chasing each other along my skin at his touch.

Bitter shame washes through me. I lean away from him, but he stops me, wrapping his arm around me and pinning me to his side. His warm, masculine scent surrounds me, but I hold my body stiffly against his.

"If I didn't find a way to pay off the debt, Ivan would have killed my whole family," I say defiantly.

"That wasn't an insult. Your family's lucky you were willing to do something so selfless to save them. Auctioning yourself off the way you did took guts. If I had that option, I would have taken it."

"So, what happened to your family?" I ask, sensing that there's more to the story.

"When my dad couldn't pay, men showed up. They carved me up in front of my dad, hoping it would convince him to miraculous produce money he didn't have. When that didn't work, they raped my mom and beat her to death. Then they went to work on my dad... they had to make an example of him, a warning to anyone else who thought they could get away without paying. My little sister ran to him to try to save him, and they killed her too."

I bite my lip to hold back a gasp, instinctively leaning further into his warmth.

"If I had just sent my mom and sister off to Chicago without me," he says, his voice laced with guilt. "I had enough money for two tickets. But I wanted to leave with them. I wanted to get us all out together. If I had just stayed behind, sent them away without me, they'd both be alive."

When I can find my voice, I say gently, "You couldn't have known what would happen. Who could've predicted that?"

He shrugs, but remains quiet.

"I'm so sorry, Dmitry. So sorry you had to go through that. But it's not your fault," I press. "You were only a child. You weren't responsible for them."

He shrugs again, and I know he doesn't believe me.

"So what about you?" I ask, changing the subject. "Why'd they let you live?"

"They didn't mean to. There was so much damage, I guess they assumed I'd bleed out. And I would have, too, if the neighbors hadn't heard the commotion and called the cops. I spent a month in the hospital, being sewn back together. Of course, all the surgeries in the world couldn't save me from looking like some fucked up Frankenstein monster." His voice is even, as if it doesn't matter to him what he looks like, but I can tell it does. It's why he carved that statue. It's how he sees himself. As an animal. A beast.

This is the first time he's told me anything personal, the first time he's dropped his guard, letting me see the man behind the scars and the mob connections and the expensive suits.

Sympathy floods me for the pain he suffered at so young an age. He didn't just lose his family; he was forced to watch as they were beaten, raped, and killed. My heart weeps for the broken child who was tortured by those animals and left for dead.

And worse yet, those monsters etched those awful memories into his skin, reminding him every day of that horrific day, of the family he lost.

Turning to face him, I respond to his last comment. "I don't think you're a monster."

"You don't have to lie to me. I know what I look like."

"No, I don't think you do," I say, studying his guarded expression. "I mean, sure, when I first saw you, I thought you were intimidating as hell. But your scars were only part of that. Mostly, it was your size, and your angry scowl. But your scars don't bother me." I reach up to brush my fingers against his cheek. "They're a part of who you are. And I think you're beautiful."

His eyes are still skeptical. I can tell he doesn't believe me. To prove I mean what I say, I lean up and press my lips against his. He's stiff at first, unresponsive. I run my tongue along his lower lip, my hands gripping his broad shoulders, exploring the hard ridges of muscles.

He groans, finally giving in. His tongue plunders my mouth, need rising swiftly in us both. A craving more potent than anything I've felt before overtakes my body. A deep need to be close to him, to crawl into his damaged soul and heal him from the inside out.

My hands slide down to his bare chest, caressing the raised, puckered lines—mementos of untold horrors no child should endure. Unable to help myself, I brush my lips lightly along the mark on his cheek.

He freezes, every muscle becoming stone, but I continue. I kiss each scar on his beautiful face, wanting to erase every moment of pain and suffering from his past.

Chapter 15

DMITRY

Her kiss undoes me. It's unfathomable that she could touch my ruined face, kiss my ugly scars, and tell me I'm beautiful.

I know I'm not. I know I'm a beast, inside and out. But for this moment, I allow myself to pretend.

Her hands clutch at my back, pulling me closer.

"Fuck, Daisy," I say raggedly, leaning my forehead against hers. "You have no idea what you do to me."

I capture her mouth with mine again, sweeping my tongue inside and tangling it with hers. She lets out a low moan, her hands fumbling with the button on my slacks.

I tear at her shirt, just as desperate. I strip her of her shirt, forcing myself to slow down, to savor each part of her body. My hands cup her breasts, rolling her tight little nipples between my fingers, eliciting a low groan. I suck her perfect tit into my mouth, teasing and tasting as she writhes and whimpers against me.

"So fucking beautiful," I tell her. "And all mine,"

"Dmitry," she says on a gasp. "God, that's amazing. You're amazing."

I slip my fingers into her wet channel, testing to see if she's ready for me. As much as I want to savor this, to etch every fucking moment in my memory for all time, I can feel my control slipping. She's driving me out of my mind.

"Do you want me?" I can't stop myself from asking. Demanding. "Tell me you want me."

"I want you, Dmitry. God, I want you. Please," she begs, her hips gyrating against my hand in mindless need.

I lift her so she's sitting on my workbench and line up my aching cock with her slick entrance. I watch her face as I slowly sink into her. Inch by inch, I slide into her waiting heat.

Her mouth opens on a wordless groan, her lashes fluttering, but she never breaks eye contact. And somehow, that feels more intimate than the interlocking of our bodies. I'm so used to hiding in shadows, avoiding human contact. But here, in this moment, I don't want to hide. I want her to see me, to see past my broken exterior to the man underneath. And I need to see her. I want to penetrate not just her body, but her very soul. I want to reach inside and weld her soul to mine, making it impossible for her to ever leave me.

Her pussy walls squeeze around me, snapping the last of my control. My fingers dig into her hips as I thrust into her with hard, fast strokes. She cries out my name, her head tossed back, fingernails dragging down my back.

"More," she pleads wrapping her legs around my waist, taking me deeper. With a snarl, I pick her up and pin her against the wall, ensuring she has no escape from me. I slam into her over and over, like an animal in rut, her whimpers and cries spurring me on.

When I feel my balls tighten, warning me that I'm near the end of my control, I reach between us and pinch her clit.

"Come for me, Daisy," I say on a harsh grunt.

She comes apart under my touch, her scream of pleasure triggering my own orgasm. I come with a roar, her name on my lips.

I keep her locked tight against me while I pump my seed into her. When I finally set her down, she wobbles on unsteady legs. I hold her until she regains her balance, noting red marks on her hips from when I held her against the wall. I worry for a moment that I hurt her, losing control the way I did, but then she smiles up at me, her eyes sleepy and pleasure-glazed.

Relief floods me. I pick her up and carry her naked into the house, straight to my bed, where she belongs.

Chapter 16

DAISY

I wake up to the room flooded with light, my muscles sore, the way they feel after a vigorous workout.

A smile breaks across my face as I remember exactly how my muscles got in this state. Last night, Dmitry opened up to me, told me things about his past in a way I never expected from him. And then he made love to me. There's no other word for it. The sex last night wasn't like that first time on the kitchen table. This time is was sweeter. Deeper. More meaningful.

Last night, it felt like we truly connected.

I know this whole thing started under strange circumstances, but for the first time in my life I can actually picture myself in a relationship.

After watching my mom crash and burn with guy after guy, I decided early on that I didn't want any part of it. Not the all-consuming drama, not the manically high peaks where reason and logic are lost, and most especially not the inevitable pain of the messy breakup.

But for Dmitry, I just might risk it.

I roll over, reaching for him, but my hands find cool, empty sheets. Nonplussed, I pull one of his shirts over my naked body and head out of the room to find him.

On the whiteboard he's left a note: Gone for a jog. Be back soon — D

I smile to myself, picturing him glistening with sweat, those lovely muscles flexing under that bronze skin. Maybe when he gets back I can help him shower.

Humming to myself, I begin making breakfast when Dmitry's landline rings. Should I answer it? It's not like anyone knows I'm here, so it can't be for me. Unless it's Dmitry calling for me. Unsure, I answer it on the third ring.

"Hello?"

"Daisy? Is Dmitry with you right now?"

"Jeremy? How did you get this number? How do you know about Dmitry?" Did Ray tell them where I really am? Oh shit...

"It doesn't matter right now. Is he near you? Is he home?" Jeremy sounds panicked, and it takes a lot to rile up my laid-back brother.

"No, he's out right now. Jeremy, what's wrong?"

"Listen, just grab your stuff and meet me outside."

"What? What's going on?"

"Just hurry, Daisy! I'm pulling up now. Get your stuff!"

"Jeremy? Jeremy??" But he's already hung up. Not a minute later, I hear the crunch of gravel of a car coming down the long driveway.

I rush out the door and am shocked to see Jeremy pull up in my mom's beat-up sedan.

"Jeremy, what are you doing here?"

"I'm getting you out of here," Jeremy says. "Ray finally came clean about what he did to you. How he sold you like a whore. How come you didn't tell me?" His mouth thins with anger. "You know I would have rescued you from the pervert who bought you!"

"He's not a pervert, Jer. He's actually been really nice to me."

Jeremy's eyes narrow dangerously. "*Not a pervert?*" he asks incredulously. "He *bought* you!"

I take a step back from the vehemence in his voice. He's usually so easy going. I haven't seen him this enraged since that night long ago, when I was just a little girl...

I shake off the old memory before it can take hold. I have to focus on the here and now.

"Really, Jeremy. I'm fine. I swear. Yeah, Dmitry bid on me, but he's been really great to me. He paid Ray's debt, plus I'll have some left over so we won't have to worry about bills for a while. Everything is fine. I'll be back home on Friday."

"Oh, no. We are leaving *now*. I found us a place outside the city. Mom's already there waiting. We need to go, now, before the Russians find out we've skipped town."

"What are you talking about? I just told you, Dmitry paid them already."

"Just get in the car, Daisy," Jeremy says, anxiously looking around. "Hurry, before he comes back. I won't let you stay with that animal a minute longer. I'll get you away from him, away from the Russians, away from this whole God damned city."

I stand rooted to the spot. I know Jeremy is just trying to help. He thinks he's rescuing me. How could he have known that I don't need to be rescued? That I don't want to be. Not from Dmitry.

And how can I possibly explain that to him without sounding crazy? How the hell can I tell my brother that I've developed *feelings* for the man who bought me at a sex auction? God, what is wrong with me? It's sick. I know it is. But Dmitry has never hurt me. In fact, he's gone out of his way to take care of me. To make

~ 115 ~

me happy. And the thought of never seeing him again, of betraying him, especially after last night…

My gut twists sickeningly. This is insane. He's a criminal. He probably buys a girl a week at those auctions. Why would I think that the last few days together meant anything more to Dmitry than a good lay?

I know I should leave. It's what any sane person would do. But as I take that first step towards the car, guilt hits me hard. I made a deal. I can't just leave like this. It isn't right.

"What the fuck are you doing?"

I jump, the rage in Dmitry's voice making my blood run cold. He comes storming out of the woods, fury blazing from his jade eyes.

"You're leaving?" He says looking at me with a mixture of accusation and disbelief. "You're fucking leaving me?"

"What? No!" I protest, guilt pinching my stomach for even considering it. "Of course I'm not." I look to Jeremy, who's frozen near the front of the car. "I'm not leaving, Jeremy. I made a deal. We had a deal. I'll be home on Friday."

Jeremy looks frightened, staring back and forth between me and Dmitry.

"Daisy, you don't know what you're doing. We need to leave. Get in the car."

"No."

"Daisy, they'll kill you." He's pleading now. "Just get in the car. I'll hold *him* off."

The thought of my slender brother attempting to face off with the mountain that is Dmitry would be laughable if it weren't so frightening. What is he thinking? Dmitry outweighs him twice over.

Some of the fury leaves Dmitry's face. Amusement lurks in his eyes, quickly suppressed.

"You should be scared, Jeremy. Ivan Vasilek isn't a man you want to betray."

Jeremy's eyes open wide. "You - you don't know what you're talking about," he says, his voice shaking.

"Oh, but I do. Why don't you tell your sister why the Russians would be coming after your family again, so soon after I paid off Ray's debt?"

I look back and forth between them, confused. Then Jeremy's face flushes with guilt, and the pieces start fitting together.

"No, Jeremy. Tell me it's not true. Tell me you didn't borrow money from them."

"It's not what you think," he hurries to say. "I wasn't gambling or anything. Ray got drunk the other night and told us what he did to you. I knew, then, that I had to get us away from him. It's only a matter of time before he racks up an even greater debt that you'd take upon yourself to pay. I couldn't let him turn you into a whore. So I borrowed some money. Enough to get us out of town. By the time the Russians come to collect it, we'll be gone. Ray's still in the city, on a bender. The Russians will go after him, and Ray will finally have to answer for his own debts. But we need to leave now! Before they realize we're gone."

"What?!" I shriek. "How could you be so irresponsible?" Behind me, I hear Dmitry growl his agreement. "Jeremy! That isn't how it works! You can't just borrow money and skip town! What, you think you're the only one to ever think of doing that? You're talking about the *mob*, Jer! They're not just going to let you go. They'll follow you! They'll find you. Jesus!"

I pace a few steps away and cover my face with my hands. I can't believe he did this. I had everything under control. I had the debt paid. I even had enough for us to leave, to get away from Ray, to start over new somewhere else. And now this!

"No, Daisy. Trust me. We'll be fine. By the time they start looking for us, we'll be long gone. They won't find us—"

"How much?" I interrupt, my face still in my hands. "How much do you owe?" Maybe the money from Friday's auction will be enough to cover it. It would screw up my plan to leave out of town, but better that than dead.

When Jeremy doesn't answer, I lower my hands to look at him. His face is drained of color, eyes wild.

"Fifty grand," Dmitry says when Jeremy stays mute. "He owes fifty thousand dollars to Ivan by Saturday morning."

"Fifty thousand?" I gasp, covering my mouth in horror. "Oh, God, Jeremy. What are we supposed to do? I just paid off Ray's debt. Even with the money I made off that auction, there's no way I can cover fifty grand!" I say with an edge of hysteria to my voice. "Even if I were to auction myself again on Friday, I'm no longer—" I look at Jeremy uncomfortably. "I won't be able to get nearly as much money this time around," I amend.

Jeremy's eyes narrow as he looks at Dmitry, but before he can say anything, Dmitry takes a threatening step towards him.

"Do you have any idea what the Bratva does to people who get into debt like that with them and don't pay? Do you? You can't run from them. You don't control a city by being stupid. They will hunt you down. They will find you. And when they do, they will make you pay for giving them so much trouble. They will make you suffer. You and your entire family. Death will be a blessing after they get through with you. Your mutilated bodies will stand as a warning to all the other dumb-shits who think they can pull one over on them."

As he says this, my gaze is drawn to the scars crisscrossing his bare chest. They'll make examples of us the same way his father's bookies made an example of him.

Jeremy's angry expression crumples into disbelief, then despair. It really never occurred to him that the Russians would continue to hunt for us after we left the city. He seriously thought we would be able to run away with their money.

"And even if you did get away, what then?" Dmitry continues, relentless. "Where would you go? What would you do? How do you plan on taking care of Daisy and your mother when you've never held a job in your life? Or were you just planning on having Daisy and your mom work full time to pay for your rent and your food while you sit around on your ass again?"

"Dmitry," I gasp. I may be pissed off, and I can't say I haven't had similar thoughts in the past, but now isn't the time for this kind of lecture. I can see on Jeremy's face how much he regrets what he did. I don't want to make him feel worse. It doesn't help anything.

"It's time to grow up," Dmitry continues. "Be a fucking man. Take care of your family."

"I'll get a job," Jeremy says, flushing. "You're right. I know I can't rely on them to do everything for me. Not again. I'll get a job this time. Things will be different. But first we need to get away, before the Russians come for us. We just have to get away."

"The Russians won't be coming for you," Dmitry says, jaw still set in anger.

"How do you know? They're not going to just forgive fifty grand."

"I paid your debt yesterday." Dmitry's talking to Jeremy, but his gaze is locked on mine.

I stare at him, shocked, unable to believe what he just said. "You paid Jeremy's debt? Why?"

Dmitry continues staring at me, and for just a moment, his intimidating mask slips, giving me a glimpse of the man he was last night. Open. Vulnerable. Tender. Then it's gone, leaving nothing but fierce possessiveness in its place.

"If I didn't pay the debt, Viktor was going to collect it from you personally. I couldn't let that happen. You're mine."

I stare at him, at a loss for words. *His.* The word sends a warm tingle all the way down my spine. Is it possible that somehow Dmitry does care about me? That he might want me for more than just sex? Maybe I'm not the only one starting to develop feelings. If Dmitry didn't care about me beyond sex, why would he care whether Viktor forces me into his bed or not?

"Yours?" Jeremy says, face twisting in disgust and barely contained anger. "She doesn't belong to you. You're just the freak who bought my sister at a sex auction!"

"No, I'm the man who just saved your life and the life of your entire family."

Jeremy opens his mouth to retort, but I jump in, cutting him off. "He's right Jeremy. If it weren't for him, all of us would be dead right now. He saved us. Twice."

"How the hell do you even know if he's telling the truth? He just *happened* to hear about my debt and pay it off right when I show up to take you away? Convenient."

"I trust him," I say, though a sliver of doubt niggles at the back of my brain. Jeremy's right—it is convenient...

"You're seriously going to take that pervert's word for it?" Jeremy asks. "We've dealt with scumbags like him all our lives. You know they can't be trusted."

"He isn't the same as mom's boyfriends. You have no idea what you're talking about."

"You can't trust him. You don't know anything about him. Just get in the car, Daisy. Please. We need to go."

Chapter 17

DMITRY

My fists ball at my sides, rage and fear threatening to choke me. If Daisy chooses to leave now, to go on the run with her family, I'll never get her back. I can't let Jeremy take her away, but short of physically dragging her inside, I don't see how I can stop it.

I watch in trepidation as Daisy looks from her brother to me, deciding. Then she crosses her arms, her chin jutting out stubbornly, and says, "No. I made a deal. I'm not leaving yet."

The shock is so strong I feel like the air has been knocked out of my lungs. She's staying? She isn't jumping on this chance to get away from me?

Jeremy looks as surprised as I feel. He steps back, reeling.

"You've got to be kidding, Daisy! He bought you like a whore! You're choosing to stay with him? When did you become mom?"

Color rises in her cheeks, but rather than back down, she spits out, "About the same time you turned into Ray! Seriously, Jeremy, how could you have put us even further into debt? I never thought I'd have to worry about that sort of thing from *you*."

"Daisy," Jeremy's voice takes on a hint of panic now. "Just trust me on this, okay? Get in the car."

"Jeremy," she sighs, exasperated. "If Dmitry says it's safe, then it is. Go back home. Everything's fine. I'm fine. I'll be back in a few days."

I study Jeremy with narrowed eyes. He has the same panicked stricken, desperate look I've seen in too many men over the years. The debt to Ivan is paid, so why is he still so scared? "What aren't you telling her?" I demand. He's hiding something. I'm sure of it.

Jeremy's jaw juts out stubbornly, just like his sister's. "It's none of your business."

"Who else is after you?" I persist. His eyes open wide for a moment, and I know my strike landed home. "Who else do you owe?"

Jeremy looks away, guilt suffusing his face.

"Jeremy?" Daisy asks, her eyebrows rushing together, creating a little 'v' of concern on her forehead.

"The Italians... and the South Side Gang," Jeremy confesses.

"Christ," I say. "How much you owe?"

He hesitates. "Fifteen thousand to the Italians, and about five to South Side."

Daisy gasps, breathing his name disapprovingly. "How could you? What would you have possibly needed all that money for?"

"It isn't cheap, going on the run. We needed gas and food and plane tickets to get us far away from here, money for hotels, and eventually rent, plus Ray stole a large chunk of my loan from the Russians. Bastard found the wad of cash in my wallet right before mom threw him out for what he did to you... Shit Daisy, the payments are due in a few days. I expected to be across the country by now, but it took me longer than I expected to find where he stashed you," he says, nodding his head toward me. "Mom is already gone —I sent her to Aunt Linda's. After I get you, we'll pick her up and just keep driving for a few states before hopping on a plane anywhere we want."

"She's staying," I growl. Fucking kid is an idiot if he thinks he can outrun the Italians. They have connections in every city from here to Vegas. I won't let Daisy get caught up in his idiotic plan.

Jeremy's eyes shoot daggers at me. "This is more important than your need to get laid. They'll kill her if she stays."

"I'll keep her safe. No one will touch her."

Jeremy casts an appraising gaze over me, lingering at the scars clearly displayed on my bare chest.

"He's right, Jer," Daisy says. "I'll be safe with Dmitry. Then, once my week is up, I'll meet up with you and mom."

I grind my teeth at her last statement. I can't let her go. I intended to tell her I'd pay Jeremy's debt if she stayed longer, but I fucked up and already admitted to paying Ivan. Now I have no leverage, no way to make her stay.

"You don't happen to have any extra money, do you?" Jeremy asks Daisy. "I left my stash with mom and am running low on gas."

And that's when I see red.

"Are you fucking kidding me?! After everything she did to buy your family's way off the Bratva's hit list, you go and run up debts with the three most dangerous groups in the whole God damned city? And then you have the fucking balls to ask her for more money?" I'm so incensed I stalk forward without meaning to. Jeremy huddles against the side of the car as I tower over him. "Daisy is already here paying one debt that isn't hers. Now you want her to pay another? You made this fucking mess, you figure out how to fix it!"

"It's ok, Dmitry," she says, her small hand reaching out to rest on my bicep. "Here." Daisy hands Jeremy a wadded up ball of cash. "It's all I have until Viktor gives me the rest of the money from the auction."

Jeremy's face brightens, despite the fact that he's still pinned between me and the car. "Thanks, sis. And I really am sorry about all of this. I was an idiot. I know that. I'll make this right, somehow. Just stay safe until you can get to us. I'll call you with the address once we find a place."

Then it hits me. Daisy will do anything to keep her family safe, and Jeremy's half-cocked plan doesn't stand a chance of working. But I could fix that...

"No," I growl. "I won't let you kill her."

Jeremy's about to argue when I reach under the wheel-well, sliding my hand under it until I find what I'm looking for.

I pull the tracking device out and hold it up so he can see. We use similar devices to keep an eye on flight risks. This proves that the Italians are watching Jeremy very closely. It won't be easy making him and his mom disappear, but I'm confident I can pull it off, with the right incentive...

"It seems the Italians are already onto you. Did you really think they'd just let you slip away? You have no fucking idea who you're dealing with. And your mom—you sent her to your aunt's house? Seriously? Friends and family are the first fucking place they'll look. All you did was guarantee that your aunt will join you in the grave."

Daisy pales, eyes locked on the small black device in my hands.

"Unless I help you, that is."

Daisy turns to me, hope shining in her eyes.

"I can get your brother and mom away from here," I tell her. "I can set them up somewhere safe. Somewhere the Italians will never find them."

"You can? You would do that?"

"Yes, if..."

"If what?" she asks, her eyes searching mine.

"If you agree to stay here." There. I said it.

Her eyes cloud over, confusion creasing her brow. "Stay? For how long?"

"Forever." My heart feels like it will pound straight out of my chest, especially when her face contorts in horror.

"You can't…You can't be serious." She takes a step away from me, fear crystalizing in her eyes. "I can't stay here *forever*. That's crazy!"

"Fine. A year," I quickly counter. The last thing I want is to scare her away. A year is better than nothing. And who knows, maybe after that I'll be able to find another enticement. Hell, with enough money, I might be able to drag this out for years and years.

"No way," Jeremy says, leaping to her defense. "You can't keep her prisoner here. That is so fucked up."

"She's safer here with me than anywhere else. I can protect her from the Italians and South Side. If she goes along with your half-cocked plan, she will end up dead. You all will. You want her to clean up your mess again? This is the price."

Turning away from Jeremy's livid expression, I look at Daisy. She seems less terrified now. Her eyes are narrowed, as if weighing all the possible consequences.

"As long as you're here, I'll take care of your family," I promise. "I'll find them a safe place to live, pay all their bills. They'll want for nothing, as long as you're here. After a year, if you want to leave, you can. Just give me a year."

Her face softens. She steps forward and reaches out to my cheek, the one with the scar. "Okay," she agrees, eyes staring into mine, fingers tracing the deep groove. "I'll stay for a year."

"You don't have to do this," Jeremy pleads with her. "We'll figure something else out; we always do."

"Do you have twenty grand to pay off the Italians and South Side? No, this is the only way. I'll stay."

Chapter 18

DAISY

Dmitry left hours ago to take Jeremy and my mom to safety. With him gone, I now have time to sit and think about what I so impulsively agreed to.

An image of how he looked when he asked me to stay pops into my mind. Despite the hard expression, his eyes were wide; vulnerable. There was the barest hint of pleading in his voice that shook me to my core. When he looked at me like that, how could I say no? Especially after he admitted to clearing Jeremy's debt with the Russians.

Why would he do that? And why would he ask me to stay? He could have just went and bought another virgin off the auction block, for considerably less money and trouble than me. Doesn't he do that all the time? The cosmetics in his bathroom certainly make it appear so. So why ask *me* to stay? Why put himself at risk like that?

Despite my best efforts, a smile breaks free, spreading across my face. He must have feelings for me. It's the only explanation. And though I've tried to fight it, I finally admit to myself that I care about him, too. More than care. I've never felt this way about anyone before. I think I might be... in love with him.

And that thought chases the silly grin from my face,

Is Jeremy right? Am I becoming my mother? Am I so blinded by love that I'm oblivious to the red flags and warning signs?

I've always wondered how my mom could go from one horrible man to the next, each time with glowing cheeks and shining eyes, every time thinking that *this* time things will turn out differently. Truly believing that this man isn't like the others; he won't lie or steal or cheat on her. He won't shoot up or drink himself into a stupor every night.

And no matter how many times it's happened, she still runs head-first into the next relationship, naive and hopeful every single time.

But after this past week with Dmitry, I think I finally understand. Love isn't something you can argue away. It doesn't listen to logic or reason. Love is illogical. Irrational. Insane.

It can't be contained, can't be controlled. It breaks all binds, disrupts the steadiest of tempers, melts even the most cynical of hearts.

Love will break you and remake you in ways you never thought possible.

I never expected to fall for Dmitry like this. But I did. And now I'm stuck in the same impossible situation my mom always finds herself in.

What the hell am I going to do?

But what happened to my mom over and over again won't happen to me, I tell myself. Her boyfriends were all users. Lowlifes who, at their best, dragged her heart around and stomped on it, and at their worst, preyed on her children. But Dmitry isn't like that. He won't hurt me. He's done everything in his power to protect me. He'll keep me safe.

For a brief time yesterday, he let me slip behind the wall he's built around himself. Allowed me to catch a glimpse of the broken child he once was, of the vulnerable man that hides behind his intimidating mask. And that man he showed me, the one so driven to protect those he cares about? That's a man worth loving.

Dmitry said he wouldn't be back until late, so I curl up on his side of the bed, dressed in another one of his shirts since I forgot, once again, to bring up my lack of clothing problem. But now that I've agreed to stay here for a year, the clothing situation needs to be rectified. When he returns, I'll ask if we can pick up my bag from Iniquity and stop by my house to get the rest of my belongings. It looks like I'll be moving in with him.

I smile and snuggle deeper into the voluminous shirt, inhaling his rich, masculine scent. I've gotten used to wearing Dmitry's clothes over the past few days, and now with him gone, wearing his shirt makes me feel like a part of him is still here with me.

Stupid, I chastise myself. He's only been gone a few hours. Silly to be missing him already. I just don't like sleeping alone in an empty house out here in the middle of nowhere. That's all it is...

I'm jolted awake the next morning by a loud banging coming from the front door. Fearing the worst, I leap out of bed and sprint for the living room. It's barely light out, dawn only just beginning. If I weren't so sleep-addled and frightened for my family, I never would have opened the door without first looking to see who it was.

The moment the door swings in, dread pools in my stomach, bile rising to the back of my throat.

Viktor. Oh God.

I hastily try to close the door, but he shoves his way in easily, cruel amusement in his gaze as it travels down my body. I pull the two gaping edges of Dmitry's shirt closer together, hands fisting protectively in front of my chest. My toes curl under his insulting inspection.

"Well, well, well. Don't you look well-used this morning?"

My mind whirls a mile a minute, heart beating out of my chest. I can't believe I opened the door. How could I have been so stupid? Jeremy just told me the Italians and the South Side Gang are looking for us. Why would I have opened the door without checking first?

Looking up into Viktor's leering, angry eyes, I'd think I'd prefer the Italians to him right now. The hatred and jealousy burning in his gaze sends prickles of alarm down my spine. The vulnerability of being here, alone with him, takes me back to a time when I was a little girl, alone in my room, at the mercy of another snake just like him. Jeremy was there to rescue me then. But I'm all alone now. Jeremy's gone. So is Dmitry. Who will save me this time?

My hands fist at my sides, anger beating back the fear.

I'll save myself.

If he makes one move toward me, I'll ram my knee through his balls. I won't let him touch me.

"So where is the beast that's been ravaging you?" he asks with a sneer. "Still in bed, recovering from your dedicated ministrations? Don't worry, sweet Daisy." He reaches out to touch my face. I smack his hand away. He smiles. "Pretty soon, you'll be free of that animal. Then you and I can have some fun. I'll treat you good," he says, a cruel smile stretching his lips. "I'll show you what a real man is like."

Gathering my courage, I brace myself, preparing to strike out with my knee as he leans closer toward me.

"What the fuck are you doing here?!" Dmitry roars, bursting through the open door. He grabs Viktor by his throat and slams him up against the wall.

Viktor's feet clear the ground, kicking uselessly. His fingers tug at the hand wrapped around his throat, to no avail. His eyes bulge wide, face turning bright red, then purple, as he tries and fails to get oxygen to his lungs.

Dmitry!" I cry, terrified at the way Viktor's eyes are bulging from his head.

He glances over his shoulder at me. I flinch back at the look on his face.

He's going to kill him.

Oh, my God. Dmitry is really going to kill him.

Dmitry's face could be carved out of granite for all the emotion on it. His eyes are hard and blank like stone. I take a slow step back, easing away from them.

Seeing this, his mouth twitches. The first cracks in Dmitry's demeanor begin to appear. He blinks, and his eyes change from glassy blankness to burning rage. Turning back to Viktor, Dmitry slams his head against the wall again and leans in close.

"You don't fucking look at her, you got that?" he snarls, his face inches from Viktor's. "Not one fucking glance."

Then Dmitry releases him, tossing him onto the floor like a piece of garbage.

Viktor coughs and sputters on the ground, catching his breath. When he finally climbs to his feet, I expect him to try to attack Dmitry, or at the very least threaten him, but he surprises me by laughing.

"She's really gotten under your skin, hasn't she? I can't wait to get under hers…"

"What are you doing here?" Dmitry says coldly, positioning his body between mine and Viktor's.

Even though Dmitry seems more in control of himself now, my heart still pounds in remembered fear at the look on his face, the cold, hard eyes.

He was ready to kill him.

It's never been more apparent how dangerous Dmitry truly is. He's a criminal. And somehow, over the last few days, I've forgotten that.

What is Dmitry's connection to Viktor and the Russian mob? He's never come right out and said, and I've been too afraid to ask. But he must have some close connection with them have heard about my brother's debt so soon and stop them from coming for us.

And if I'm going to be staying here for the next year, I need to know exactly what it is.

"Ivan's called a meeting for tomorrow. I came by to inform you personally. He wants an update on your..." he looks at me, then glances back to Dmitry. "He wants an update on your pet project."

"You could have called," Dmitry says, still blocking him from me.

"Yeah, well I also brought this." Viktor motions to a bag on the floor I hadn't noticed until now, the same bag I left at Iniquity the night of the auction. "I thought little Daisy here might need it. Plus, I wanted to make sure you haven't roughed her up too badly. I don't want her too damaged. A little bruised is okay, though." His lips pull into another cruel smile.

Dmitry growls low in his throat. I reach out and wrap a hand around his bulging forearm to stop him from attacking him again.

"No need to get so riled. She's just a whore you paid for. If I offer her enough money, I'll bet she lays back and spreads them for me right here and now."

"Never," I spit out, moving closer to Dmitry's back.

"Everybody has their price, sweet Daisy," he says. "Or hasn't your brother told you about the newest debt your family has accumulated? But don't worry; I'll let you work it off for me personally." He winks.

My stomach heaves, imagining Viktor in bed with me, forcing himself inside of me.

No. Never. Not even for my family would I let that monster touch me.

"Didn't you hear?" Dmitry asks, his voice deceptively pleasant. "That debt has already been paid, and Ivan has given strict orders that we're not to lend any more money to their family, for any reason. So, it looks like Daisy will be staying here for the time being. Now get the fuck out."

Viktor's gloating expression disappears. His face hardens, rage lighting his eyes. He glares at me, then Dmitry, before turning on his heel and slamming the door behind him.

My body goes weak. I stumble backwards and collapse on the couch, my legs no longer able to support me.

"What the hell was that?" I ask, my hands still shaking after their brutal confrontation. "How do you know him, Dmitry? What's your connection to the head of the Russian Mob?"

"It's better for you if you don't know." He watches out the window until Viktor's shiny black sports car disappears from view. "I'm sorry that he came by here like this. It won't happen again."

He walks over to the computer desk, pulling a keyring from his pocket. Unlocking the top drawer, he takes something out of it, but I can't see what it is until he's sitting next to me again.

I leap away from the gun he's extending out towards me as if it were a snake.

"What the hell?" I say, fleeing to the other side of the room.

"I want you to keep this on you at all times when I'm not home."

"No. No way. Get that thing away from me. And don't try to brush me off about the Russians. If you want me to stay here for the next year, I need to know what I'm getting into. Do you work for him? Are you actually part of the mob?"

"Daisy, the less you know the better. I'm trying to protect you."

"The best way to protect me is to *tell me the truth*. How do you know Ivan? You two seemed pretty close the night of the auction. I didn't think to ask earlier. I didn't want to ask. But now I need to know. I need you to be honest with me."

Dmitry gives me a look, his eyes searching mine, as if gauging my determination. Whatever he finds seems to convince him.

He sets the gun onto the coffee table and approaches me slowly, his hands out to his side as if not to spook me. It's only then that I realized I've been slowly backing away from him.

"All right," Dmitry says, closing the distance between us. "All right. I'll tell you. Do you remember I said that I was found by the police and sent to the hospital? What I didn't tell you is that Ivan visited me while I was there. Apparently, he knew my dad. He told me that my dad had gotten in deep with the Italians. They were the ones who came to my house that night. Ivan said that in honor of his friendship with my dad, he would do what he could to look after his only surviving child.

"Ivan paid all of my hospital bills, and for my physical therapy afterward. And when I was released from the hospital, he took me home with him. He raised me as his own. He was worried the Italians might still come after me, to tie up 'loose ends'.

"If it wasn't for Ivan, I don't know what would have happened to me. He saved my life."

I listen to Dmitry's story, my hands clenched tight in my lap. All the pieces begin to fall into place. That's how Dmitry's involved with the Russians. Ivan Vasilek saved his life. He *raised him as his own*. Dmitry grew up as an intimate member of the largest crime syndicate family in the tri-state area.

Jesus. And I thought my mom had bad taste in men?

Panic threatens to overwhelm me. He's a criminal. I knew he was a criminal. But, *fuck*... I had no idea just how deep in it he was.

"So, what? You work for Ivan now?"

"Yeah," he says, studying my face with worried eyes. "I began working for Ivan from the time I was eleven. Started out running errands and such. Making drops. It was the only way to pay him back for all he had done for me."

"But that's not what you do for him now, is it? Errands?"

"No."

He doesn't elaborate, so I press him. "What do you do for him, now?"

Dmitry avoids my eyes, looking out across the room. "I do what needs to be done," he says, his jaw set.

"What does that mean?"

"Daisy, it's the Bratva. What do you think I do?"

"You beat people up for money they owe?"

He doesn't deny it.

"Just like those thugs who beat you up for your dad's debt? Who killed your family? Jesus, Dmitry, how could you?"

Anger flashes across his face. "I've never tortured a child or murdered a family like those fucking Italians did to me."

"But you *have* killed people, haven't you?" I ask, refusing to back down. "As you said, it's the Bratva. They don't just beat people up. They *kill* people. Is that what you do for them? You're their hit man?"

Dmitry looks away again, refusing to meet my glare.

"Jesus, you have." My stomach rolls sickeningly. "You've killed people."

I turn away abruptly, needing space.

"Daisy," Dmitry calls, but I ignore him. I'm running for the front door before I realize I've moved. I have to get out of here. I need to get away from him. Away from this entire fucked up situation.

God, I'm an idiot. Such a fucking idiot.

How could I have fallen in love with a killer?

Chapter 19

DMITRY

She's gone. She left me. Couldn't stand to be in the same room as me once she found out what I was.

I shouldn't be surprised. I know what I am. I knew she would leave once she knew. But I had hoped.

Hope. How fucking stupid. I should know better by now. Where the fuck has hope ever gotten me? I had hoped my deadbeat father would stop drinking. Hoped he'd stop beating me and my mom and my sister every night. I hoped to protect them, to get them out of the city before his addiction ruined us all.

But he never stopped drinking or using. Never stopped hurting us. And my mom and sister never got out of that shithole. They died there, butchered like animals because of my fucking *hope.*

No, hope has never done a damn thing for me.

I stand by the door and watch Daisy take off running into the forest.

If I was smart, I'd let her go. I'd drop her off with her brother and mom, get them far away from me and this miserable city, and hope that she stays safe from the Italians and everyone else looking to hurt her.

But hope has never gotten me anywhere before. I won't trust in it now.

No, the only way to keep her safe is if she's with me, where I can protect her. Even if that means she'll hate me for it. I'll just have to learn to live with her hatred, because I'm not letting her go.

My mind made up, I take off into the forest after her.

DAISY

I bolt through woods, leaves and branches whipping my face and tangling in my hair. Tears stream down my face, blurring my vision. Fear is a living, breathing animal trying to escape through my chest. I trip a few times, thick mud sticking to my bare legs. How could I have let this happen? He's a hit man. A killer. He is so much worse than anyone my mom ever dated. And I judged her for bad taste? Unbelievable.

I need to leave. That's the only thought in my head. But where can I go? My family is hidden away somewhere only Dmitry knows, and I have two separate gangs hunting for me back in the city. Three now, I assume, since Dmitry is part of the Russian syndicate and I technically ran off without paying my debt. I promised him I'd stay another year in exchange for him keeping my family safe. What will happen to them if I leave?

I slow my pace, my initial flare of fear beginning to cool. I agreed to stay with him. I sold myself off to the highest bidder like a whore, in order to pay my family's debt. The same way Dmitry sold himself out as a hired gun to save his life.

I spot a road up ahead. It's quiet. Deserted. I sit on a large boulder on the side of it, wrapping Dmitry's shirt tighter around me, and wait for my heart to stop galloping.

I try to picture nine-year-old Dmitry. His family had just been brutally murdered in front of his eyes and he spent a full month in the hospital, getting patched back together after his father's enemies tortured and mutilated him. He had no money, no family, no way of paying his astronomical hospital bills. And the Italians were still gunning for him. What else could he have done? If Ivan hadn't taken him under his wing, Dmitry would have ended up dead.

Of course he would agree to run some errands for the man who saved his life. And as he grew older, the errands became more dangerous, more violent. I'd like to think that someone in that situation would refuse to hurt other people. Refuse to kill other people. But realistically, what other choice would a child have? An adolescent? He was raised in a family where violence and bloodshed was a regular part of life. It makes sense that he would think such things are normal. That he would grow up to be what he is: a killer.

Looked at from this perspective, I can't blame him for how he was raised. For what he became.

But that doesn't mean I can agree to be a part of it.

A pickup truck passes me by as I'm lost in thought, the first vehicle I've seen on this deserted road.

It gets about a hundred yards passed me before it stops. White reverse lights blink on, and it backs up to where I'm sitting.

"Need a ride?"

The man behind the wheel is in his forties, thick and stocky with dishwater blond hair. His dark eyes run over my body, sheathed only in Dmitry's button-up shirt. Then he scans the woods behind me, checking to see if I'm alone, before returning his gaze my bare legs peeking out below the hem of the shirt.

There's another man in the passenger seat, also staring, this one rail thin with dark, unkempt hair.

Goosebumps ripple up my arms at the excited smiles that stretch across their faces.

"We were just headed towards town if you need a lift," the blond man offers, his eyes still raking down my body. "It can be dangerous around here for a woman alone. You never know who's wandering around in these woods."

The skinny guy laughs and elbows the blond one, like he just told some hilarious joke I'm not a part of.

Alarm bells start blaring in my head. Five minutes ago, all I wanted was to get away from here, away from Dmitry, the self-professed killer.

But even though I know Dmitry has killed people, I've never been truly frightened of him. Not the way I am of these two. I've never once felt as if I was in danger with Dmitry. The opposite, in fact. He's gone out of his way to make me feel safe, to protect me and care for me.

And yet, he kills people for a living.

I can't reconcile *my* Dmitry—the one who looks at me so tenderly when we make love, who creates such beautiful works of art with his hands, who spirited my family away to safety and paid my brother's debt without a second thought just to keep me safe— I can't reconcile that Dmitry with the one who murders people for the Russian Mob.

While these thoughts are going through my head, the driver's side door opens and the big blond man gets out. Panic blasts through me.

Shit! The other guy is getting out too. I hastily look around, hoping by some miracle that Dmitry will materialize in front of me. But he doesn't. I ran away from him. I left him, abandoned him after everything he's done for me and my family, and now I'm out in the middle of nowhere with these two terrifying men who are slowly stalking toward me.

Adrenaline courses through my veins. My muscles bunch, preparing to sprint into the woods. But before I make it, I'm grabbed from behind. A beefy hand covers my mouth before I can scream.

I kick and thrash, trying to throw the larger man off.

"Easy, there, girl. Take it easy. We won't hurt you," he says from behind me, chuckling and pulling my body tight against his. I can feel his erection through the thin material of Dmitry's shirt. "We'll take good care of you," he says, punctuating his words with a crude thrust of his hips against my backside.

Fear threatens to choke me. I let my body go limp for a moment, catching him off guard. When he adjusts his stance to catch me, I slam my head back with as much force as I can muster, crushing his nose with the back of my skull.

He roars in pain, dropping me. I roll once, frantically trying to get my bearings.

"You bitch!" he screams, hands cupping his bloody face. "You're gonna fucking pay for that. Grab her, Sal!"

Just as I climb to my feet, fire ignites in the back of my scalp. Sal yanks a handful of my hair back, making me stumble.

"We'll show you, you stupid cunt. You can't fight us. You think you're the first slut who thinks she's better than us? We'll show you who the fuck is in charge!"

My back slams into the hard earth. Sal's wiry body is surprisingly strong. He pins me to the ground underneath him, one of his hands clamped around both my wrists. The other roves hand my body, squeezing my breast before sliding further downward.

Terror paralyzes me.

This can't be happening.

Oh, God. Not again.

The past sucks me down into its dark abyss, and suddenly I'm ten years old again.

The monster's face looms above mine, hidden in shadow. All except his eyes. Those dark, snake-like eyes, reflected in the dim light from the nightlight. A finger rises to his smiling lips.

"Shhhh…"

Then I'm back in the present, and another monster looms above me. Different, but still the same. His hand fumbles at the waistband of his jeans.

I shriek and fight against his hold, beyond fear, beyond terror. I buck and thrash for all I'm worth, but his weight keeps me firmly trapped.

This is it, I think. They're going to rape me. They'll probably kill me afterward. I left Dmitry, abandoned him, ran away from the one person who's promised to keep me safe, and now I'm going to die here, in the middle of nowhere, trapped beneath these two animals.

One minute, my hands are pinned above my head, my chest struggling for breath beneath a crushing weight, and the next I'm staring up at the empty space above me where the monster just was.

It takes me a moment to process what happened. When I realize that I'm actually free, that he's somehow been knocked off me, I leap up and stare around in confusion.

I spot him on the ground, Dmitry leaning over him, punching him again and again and again.

His head snaps back with every hit. He isn't making any sound; he's knocked out cold. Blood is everywhere. I can barely make out the man's face in the mess.

I cry out a warning as the blond man I struck in the nose attacks Dmitry from behind. The early morning sunlight glints off the switchblade clasped in his hand.

Quicker than my eyes can follow, Dmitry spins around and strikes out, knocking the knife from his hand. Then he's on him like a wild animal, spurts of blood flying through the air as Dmitry mauls him.

I gasp, frozen to the spot, watching the onslaught as if it's happening to someone else. A strange buzzing fills my head. My body feels wobbly, like all my insides have turned to liquid. Dmitry's face whips in my direction, his eyes wide with fear, right before everything goes black.

Chapter 20

DMITRY

When I see those two animals attacking her, rage engulfs me, filling me, consuming me. My kills are always cold, always unemotional. But there's no way for me to remain emotionally detached when Daisy is involved.

I'm barely aware of what I'm doing until I hear Daisy's soft gasp. My gaze flies to her just as she loses consciousness, slumping to the ground below.

"Daisy!" I call out, abandoning the scumbag beneath me as I spring toward her. Both of the men who dared to touch her, dared to touch what's *mine*, are unconscious, though the fact that they're still breathing chafes at me. They shouldn't be allowed to live after what they just tried to do to my Daisy.

They need to fucking die.

But first, I need to make sure Daisy's alright.

I thought I got here in time. It didn't look like they had hurt her before I tore that fucker off her. Please, God, let me have gotten to her in time.

Daisy is passed out cold in the grass, my shirt still wrapped around her slender form. I delicately scoop her up into my arms, cradling her against my chest.

"Daisy, baby, can you hear me?"

She lets out a quiet moan, turning her face into my chest.

"It's alright, sweetheart. I got you. You're safe. You're alright. I got you."

She begins to stir then, her eyes slowly blinking, trying to focus.

"Dmitry?" she whispers. "You're here. You came for me."

"Yeah, baby. I'm here. I'll always come for you. You're mine," I say, unable to keep the possession from my voice. "How do you feel? Are you hurt anywhere?"

"No, I'm fine," she says, trying to sit up. "Just a little dizzy. You got here in time…" she says, her gaze dropping away from mine.

I release the breath I didn't even know I was holding.

Thank God. I got here in time.

I know the exact moment she sees the two rednecks sprawled out on the ground, a mess of blood and broken bones. She half gasps, half sobs, her hand covering her mouth.

"Oh, my God. Are they…are they alive?" she asks tentatively, her gaze shifting to me, then quickly away.

"They're alive," I answer, though every molecule in my body is screaming for me to end them. To make sure these fuckers don't witness another night on this earth. But the time for killing them is gone. I can't do it now, not with Daisy watching me. Not after she ran from me, terrified of what I am.

Then her gaze finds mine again, her eyes clearer and colder.

"But, if you let them go, what happens the next time they come across a woman? I'm pretty sure they've… hurt… women before. They'll do it again."

I study her expression, trying to read the undercurrent in her voice. Surely she's not asking me what I think she is? My gentle Daisy, so sweet and innocent, can't be asking me to kill two men in cold blood. Could she?

Her eyes remain locked on mine, unwavering.

She is. She wants them dead. She wants me to do what I so badly want to do myself.

But it isn't right. She may think this is what she wants, but following through on it would be another matter entirely. My sweet Daisy wouldn't be able to bear the guilt of those men's blood on her hands, even if it was me who did the actual killing. Just knowing she desired it would be enough. The guilt would crush her.

It's my job to protect her, even from herself.

So instead of snapping their necks as I'm itching to do, I rummage in the back of the pickup until I find some rope and duct tape. Daisy watches me, but doesn't say anything as I tie them up and take out my cell.

As I make an anonymous call to 911, informing them where to find the potential rapists, I hold Daisy's gaze, trying to gauge her reaction. Will she be annoyed or relieved that I'm not killing them as she wanted?

I hang up the phone, and a sharp knot in my chest loosens as relief crosses Daisy's face. I was right to let them live, though I may end up regretting it.

The law system in this country is seriously fucked up. Without irrefutable proof that these two were going to rape someone—which is damned hard to prove, even in cases where the rape actually takes place—these bastards will walk free.

But it will be alright. If the cops do turn these animals loose, I'll be here to take out the garbage. Their days are numbered. One way or another, they won't be preying on vulnerable women anymore. They'll either spend the rest of their days inside an 8x10 cage, or they'll spend in six feet under. I'm fine with either outcome.

Before we leave, I check the names in their wallets. Ryan Matthews and Salvatore Russo. I spend a moment committing their addresses to memory. I'll check on them in the next few days, and if they aren't locked up on other charges, I'll be paying them a visit.

Daisy is shaky, but otherwise unhurt. I carry her through the woods back to the house, even though she insists she's well enough to walk. I know she is, but after what almost happened, I need to feel her alive and well in my arms, even if she never again willingly accepts my touch. I may have saved her yet again, but I'm still the killer she ran from less than an hour ago.

I savor the trip back to the house, fully aware that these may be my last moments holding her this close. If she despises me as much as I think she does, this will be the last time she lets me touch her.

It will be torture, seeing her every day in my house but being unable to touch her, but I won't force myself on her. The deal was that she stays with me for a year. There was no mention of her having to share my bed.

When we arrive back at the cabin, I place her gingerly on the couch, then step away, giving her space.

She studies me with guarded eyes, biting her lower lip. Several minutes of silence pass before she finally breaks it.

"I'm sorry I ran."

I don't respond. I just watch her, waiting for the words that will destroy all my carefully laid plans, extinguish all my tenuous hopes for the future.

"I shouldn't have taken off," she continues when I don't respond. "It was stupid of me. I just panicked, and the next thing I knew, those men were—"

Her voice breaks on the last, tears springing to her eyes. I can't keep my distance any longer. I'm beside her in a moment, wrapping my arms around her shaking shoulders and pulling her against me, letting her sob into my chest while my hands caress her back in soothing circles.

"It's okay. You weren't stupid. You were scared. With good reason. You ran from one killer, and ended up in the clutches of two more. Christ, Daisy. When I think about what could have happened to you…" Fear chokes off the rest of my words. I clutch her more tightly to me, trying to banish the terror pulsing through my veins.

I wait for her to pull away, and after a moment, she does. Disappointment pinches in my chest, but it's no less than I expected. No less than I deserve.

I sit further back on the couch, giving her space, though every fiber of my being is screaming at me to hold her tight to make sure she's really here, safe and whole.

She wipes at her cheeks with the backs of her hands, drying her eyes before studying me once again. I have no idea what she's thinking, and I don't have the courage to ask. Any moment she will ask to leave, to retract her deal to stay here, and then I'll have to watch the inevitable hatred crystalize in her eyes when I tell her no. When I tell her that I won't allow her to leave.

"Thank you," she finally says. "For saving me. Again."

I don't respond. I just study her beautiful face, committing it to memory. This could be the last she'll sit here so close to me, the last time she'll willingly be in the same room as me or look at me like this, without fear and hatred clouding her beautiful blue eyes.

There's a good chance she'll even try to run away again. I'll have to keep a close eye on her. And if she does try to run from me, she won't get far. I'll follow her, wherever she goes. I won't let her go. The world is too dangerous a place for her.

She needs me to keep her safe.

I steel myself for the inevitable conversation.

"So, Ivan raised you?" she asks, surprising me. Of all the things I thought she'd ask, this is the last thing expected.

I pause a moment before answering, trying to figure out where she's going with this. Finally, I nod.

"And you've been his...." she trails off, searching for the right word.

"Enforcer," I supply.

"Right, um, you've been his enforcer for all this time?"

The fact that she's willing to talk about this calmly after her previous reaction might be a good sign. Maybe she's not as repulsed by me as I thought.

I squash that spark of hope before it can take root.

"Yes," I answer. "I've been his enforcer since I was a teenager."

"Jesus," she breathes. But she doesn't look scared anymore. Instead, she's back to studying me, searching for something.

I look away, unable to bear her scrutiny. "I was planning on getting out." I don't know why I tell her this. I guess some idiotic part of me is still hoping to reverse the damage I caused by admitting what I do for a living.

"I was going to leave the organization," I continue. "I had two weeks left on my contract, and then I was going to pack up and start clean somewhere else."

"You were?"

Surprise lights up her eyes, along with hope. But hope for what?

"What happened?" she asks. "What changed your mind?"

"I saw you at the auction." It's only a small lie. I first saw her much earlier than that, but the effect was the same. "I saw you, and I knew I had to have you. I could have out-bid every other man there. Every man, except Viktor. And once he saw that I wanted you, he would have spent a fortune to make sure I didn't get you."

"Why?" She leans unconsciously closer, riveted.

"Viktor has some issues with me. He's had it in for me since the moment his father took me home from the hospital."

"He's jealous of you," she says. "You took his place in his home, with his family. With his father. It was clear, even to me, that Ivan cares for you. Though I only saw you together for a few minutes, the affection between you two was obvious,"

I shrug. "By the time Ivan took me in, Viktor was already nineteen. Almost an adult. It's not like I took his father away from him." But I think back to those early years in Ivan's home; to all the times Viktor went out of his way to make my life hell. I always assumed he hated me because he thought I was pathetic. The poor, disfigured orphan boy his dad took pity on. But looking at it now through Daisy's eyes, it's possible some of his anger with me could be fueled by jealousy.

"So," she says, breaking into my reverie. "What happened at the auction? How is it you won me instead of him?"

"When I knew I couldn't outbid Viktor, I made a deal with Ivan instead."

"What kind of deal?"

"Six months," I say. "I agreed to stay on as his enforcer for six more months if he stopped the auction and gave you to me."

I see her bristle at the idea of Ivan 'giving' her to me, and I immediately regret those words. It makes her sound like an object, like a toy to be bought. Which, I suppose, is how I saw her then. I didn't really think of her as a person, as someone with her own thoughts and opinions and feelings, someone who should be able to make her own decisions. No, instead I did everything in my power to make sure she had no choice except the one I wanted her to make.

And I'm still doing it, I realize. I'm still not giving her any choice in the matter. Not really. Sure, she could have turned down my offer yesterday, just like she could have refused to sign up for the auction, but I knew she wouldn't. Not when her family's safety was at stake.

And as wrong as I know it is, I can't feel any regret for it. I can't say that I'll let her go now, that I'll give her the choice to leave me.

But I don't see her as just an object anymore. After getting to know her this past week—really getting to know her, not just watching her from afar the way I did—I know she's a person, an individual with her own hopes and dreams and desires. I don't want to take that away from her, but I can't let her go. I'm not strong enough for that.

Daisy still looks annoyed, but then her expression turns hesitant. "So, six more months? You're going to keep…working for him…for six more months?"

'Am I going to keep killing people' for six more months. That's what she's really asking.

"I do what I have to do, Daisy. I'm not proud of it. It's not like I enjoy breaking a man's kneecaps or creating widows and orphans. It's fucked up, what I do. I know that. That's why I was planning on leaving. I *am* leaving. But I made a deal, and now I have six more months added to my sentence. After that, it's over. I'm done."

Her face softens at this. Then she takes a deep breath, composing herself, and says, "Okay."

"Okay?" I ask, sure I heard her wrong.

"I understand why you did what you did. You were just a child when they recruited you. You didn't have anywhere else to go, anyone else to turn to. I get it. I don't like it," she says, her mouth twisting into a grimace. "But I get it. I mean, look what I did in order to save my family. You did what you had to do to survive."

My chest pulls tight, a strange ache forming. At least she doesn't despise me. That's something.

I turn her words over in my head, struggling to understand what she's not saying. "So, you're going to stay, then? You're not going to try to run away again, even knowing what I do? What I am?"

"No. I won't run away again," she promises. "You said you're trying to get out, right? You *are* getting out. That's what matters. Just six more months." She attempts a smile, but it wobbles. "Besides, we had a deal, right?"

She's staying. To honor the deal. I don't know why that thought should make me feel hollow. Her reason for staying shouldn't matter. I should just be grateful that she is staying, of her own free will.

But I can't help the small part of me that wants her to stay because she *wants* to; even though I know that's impossible.

Just another useless, ridiculous hope.

I know I'm not good enough for her. I know I shouldn't drag her into my world, into this hellhole that is my life, but I'm not strong enough to let her go.

I think of what could have happened if I hadn't come back when I did. I cannot believe Viktor showed up here. I didn't anticipate that. I have to be more careful from now on.

I move closer to Daisy, slowly, waiting for her to recoil from me. But she doesn't. Not until I reach for the pistol. At the site of the gun, she scrambles backwards on the sofa to get away from me.

"Get that away from me, Dmitry. I don't want it."

"Daisy, it's not going to bite you. It's just a gun. Just a tool."

"Yeah, one that can go off in my hand and kill me or anyone else around me."

"You've never held a gun before?"

"Of course not! When would I have held a gun before?"

I sigh, seeing the fear in her eyes. She just had the shit scared out of her by Viktor, and then by those two scumbags in the woods. She's had enough fear for one day.

"Fine. We won't practice with it today. But it's going to be here, in the top drawer, if you need it."

"I won't," she says.

"I'll feel better if you knew where it was, just in case." I run my hand through my hair in frustration, worry for her safety eating at me. "And what was Viktor doing in the house, anyway? Why would you open the door for him?"

"I heard someone banging on it," she says, crossing her arms defensively. "I thought it was you. I thought maybe something had happened with my family."

I blow out a breath. On top of everything else, she's been worrying about her family. I never even told her that I got them safely away. What an ass I am.

I sit down and wrap an arm around her shoulder. She holds herself stiffly, angry at my accusatory tone, I assume. Great. I just got her to not hate me, and now I'm driving another wedge between us.

"Your family is fine," I tell her. "I should have told you earlier. I got them to a safe place. They'll be fine."

She breathes out a relieved sigh. "Oh, thank God."

"I still can't believe your brother borrowed money from the Italians. It's bad enough he took out such a huge loan from us, but the fucking Italians? What the hell was he thinking?"

"Jeremy isn't known for thinking things through, but his intentions were good. He was just trying to do the same thing I was: get our family out from under Ray's debt," she says, defending him.

"By putting your family in even more danger? He's your brother. He should be looking out for you. Protecting you. And instead, you're off selling yourself at a sex auction and giving Jeremy the last bit of money in your wallet to get him out of town."

I know I'm only pushing her further away by attacking her family like this, but I can't seem to stop myself. All the anger and frustration inside of me just comes spewing out of my mouth. Everything I've held in since I've first witnessed her family's revolting lack of responsibility, or even gratitude for all the sacrifices Daisy's made for them over the years.

I can see her hackles rising, her instinctive reaction to defend her family surging to the forefront. I know my tirade isn't going to accomplish anything except to drive her further away from me, but I can't stop the damning words from spilling out. For a man who prides himself on control, my complete lack of discipline right now is appalling. But damn, whenever Daisy is involved, I lose all reason or sense.

"You even agreed to spend a full year with *me* in order to protect them. Why? You've sacrificed *everything* to take care of your family—your education, your hard-earned money, your body, even your fucking freedom!—and all they do in return is push you further into danger, then ask you for more. Why? Why do you do it?"

"Because they're my family, Dmitry." Her response is soft, quiet; so unlike the angry, defensive one I expected. "That's what family does. We protect each other."

"It seems to me you're the only one doing any sort of protecting. Ray and Jeremy sitting on their asses all day, running up debt in your family's name, while your mom parades an endless string of dirtbag boyfriends through your home..."

Just the thought of her selfish family constantly laying their problems on her shoulders has my anger bubbling to the surface again.

She makes a face at the mention of her mom. "Yeah, my mom has made some bad decisions in her life. I can't deny that. But she's always made sure we've had a roof over our heads and food on our table. More than a lot of people can say. And Jeremy... well, Jeremy looks out for me. It may not seem like it, but he does."

I raise an eyebrow skeptically.

"He does," she insists. "Back when we were younger, my mom had some really bad boyfriends. Mostly losers who drank and stole money; only a few ever hit us. But some were... worse. When I was ten, one of the men snuck into my room. He tried to... do things to me." She flinches when she says this, and my heart clenches sickeningly.

No... God, no.

The thought of Daisy, so young and innocent, left unprotected while some monster preyed on her... The thought leaves me sick and shaking.

"Jeremy heard me crying," she continues, clenching her hands tight in her lap. "He was only twelve, but he ran into my room and attacked him. Just launched himself at a fully grown man four times his size. He ended up in the hospital with fifteen stitches in his head. But even after Mark threw him across the room and split his head open, Jeremy still went after him. He was determined to get him away from my bed. He wasn't strong enough to fight him off, but the commotion was enough to wake my mom. It was enough to stop him.

"Jeremy may be immature, but his heart is in the right place."

Pain like I've never known erupts in my chest. Some bastard tried to... I can't even think the words without needing to kill someone.

"Mark what?" I ask. "What's his last name?"

Daisy eyes me worriedly. She must hear the bloodlust in my voice.

"It's not important," she says. "He went to jail for what he did to me."

"I can still get to him in there. There's nowhere on this whole God damn planet that he'll be safe from me."

I expected her to be frightened by the naked fury in my voice, but instead she looks oddly... touched.

"I heard he died a few years ago. Some inmate fight. He's gone."

I clench my jaw and try to suppress my fury. The fucker got off too easily. Much too easily. If I got my hands on him, I'd keep him alive for years. For decades. And each moment of his life would be spent in excruciating pain. The bastard had no idea how lucky he was to get murdered in prison.

I don't say any of this, of course. No need to give her any more reasons to fear me.

Instead, I say, "You've been taking care of your mom and brother your entire life. It's time someone took care of you for a change. I can do that. If you let me."

Chapter 21

DAISY

My eyes tear up at his declaration. It's probably sweetest thing anyone has ever said to me. No one has offered to take care of me before. Not even my own family. Despite my annoyance at Dmitry for criticizing my family, deep down, I know what he's saying isn't wrong. They *do* expect me to take care of them, they have for a long time. It's exhausting, holding everything together all by myself.

Dmitry's offer touches me more than I can say.

So instead of using words I can't find, I climb up onto his lap, needing to feel his body against mine. Taking his face in my hands, I lean in and softly press my lips to his.

He opens for me, his tongue gently tangling with mine. My irritation melts, turning to white-hot desire. I relax into him, pushing all of my worries and fears and nightmarish memories to the back of my mind. I kiss him deeply, my tongue exploring his mouth more aggressively than I've done before.

He pulls back, worry and lust at war in his eyes. "Are you sure about this?"

He probably wonders how I could want him this way right now, after what I just told him. Not to mention what happened in the woods.

What almost happened.

I force those memories away, focusing only on the here and now. I need him to touch me. I need him to chase away the memories still lurking at the edges of my mind, to erase the imprint of those other men's hands on me.

Even knowing now what I do about Dmitry, what he does, I still feel safer in his arms than I do anywhere else. Despite everything I've learned today, I still love him. I can't help myself.

"You don't have to do this," he continues. "Our agreement was for you to stay in this house for the next year, not my bed. I don't want anything from you that you don't want to give."

He thinks I'm only doing this because of our agreement? My heart melts at the longing in his eyes.

"I want this," I assure him. "I want *you,* Dmitry. Please."

The hard planes of his face relax, relief flooding his eyes. He kisses me softly, sweetly. His fingers lightly graze down my arms, sending delicious tingles all the way down to my toes.

When we had sex before, it was wild and intense. The fierce joining of two bodies, rough and wild and untamed. But this time is different. It's softer, sweeter, though no less intense.

He lets me take the lead this time, content to sit back as I straddle him, kissing him deeply, our mouths and lips and tongues dancing together. Playful nips and deep, husky laughs help lighten the weight that's been pressing on my chest since Jeremy showed up yesterday with his alarming news.

I slowly lower myself to the floor between Dmitry's thighs, smiling shyly up at him. His intense gaze never leaves mine.

"Take off your shirt," I tell him as I go to work on his pants. He grins at me, his expression so light and carefree I feel my heart squeeze.

"You first," he teases.

Dmitry, teasing! I never would have guessed he had this side to him, but I am delighted to have discovered it.

I grin back at him before raising my arms and slowly, teasingly, lift the shirt over my head.

His green eyes flare as they trace down my bare flesh.

"Your turn," I say as I yank his pants and boxers down. He lifts his hips to help me, but hesitates with his shirt.

He can't still be self-conscious about the scars, can he? He must know by now that they don't bother me.

I raise one eyebrow, trying to keep my tone light. "Please? I love looking at you. You're so beautiful. You have to know that."

He looks at me doubtfully, then lets out a soft gasp when I lightly rake my fingernails down the outside of his thighs.

"Pretty please?" I breathe, leaning in close so he can feel my warm breath on his shaft, standing rigidly at attention between us.

I trace the tip of his head with my tongue and watch his eyes roll back in his head. Then I sit back again, biting my lip coquettishly, still waiting for him to remove his shirt.

He gives in with a groan, tearing his shirt off in one fluid motion. My mouth waters, yearning to taste every delectable inch of his sculpted body. But I start on my favorite part, sucking him into my mouth, all the way to the back of my throat. He gasps, his hands coming up to cup my face, thumbs stroking the sides of my face while I work him with my lips and tongue.

Chapter 22

DMITRY

"Daisy, Jesus," I gasp out. "I'm going to come if you keep doing that. Fuck!" I pull her up before I explode in her mouth. "Come here, baby." I pull her against me so she's straddling my lap again. I need to feel her body against mine.

I tug her head down to mine, plundering her mouth with long, deep strokes. My hands caress the soft skin of her back and upper arms, drifting down to her firm ass. I squeeze, unable to help myself, but I allow her to take the lead once again.

She's shy, uncertain, as she lines up her entrance with my rigid shaft. My cock brushes against her warm pussy and I suck in a breath between clenched teeth.

Fuck! This woman will be the death of me. She's so hot, so innocently sexy as she fumbles with my cock, dragging my head through her wet folds. Slowly—God, so slowly!—she sinks down onto me, sheathing me in her silken heat.

Need beats at me, urging me to take control and drive into her again and again, but I restrain myself. I let Daisy set the pace, savoring every slow roll of her hips, her every soft gasp and quiet whimper.

It goes against my every instinct, giving control up to another. I'm always in control of myself, always restrained, always disciplined. Or I was, before Daisy entered my life. Now, I don't know which way is up anymore. She has my emotions bouncing all over the place, all the time. Feelings that I thought were long dead have been resurrected, and I'm not sure how I feel about any of it.

In my experience, the moment you lose control, you wind up dead. Trust is a foreign concept. And love… well, love simply doesn't exist.

But when I'm with Daisy like this, it's hard to stay in control of anything, least of all my emotions. She pulls me in, warms me up from the inside out, and lights up my dark soul with her shining innocence. She makes me hope again.

And hope can be a dangerous thing.

* * *

DAISY

We lay together, catching our breath, while my fingers idly trace the marks marring his beautiful flesh. He doesn't try to stop me, doesn't shy away from my touch, and I smile to myself.

I'm still buzzing from the intense orgasm he wrung from me. I never imagined how exhilarating being in control like that could be. It's a heady feeling. Powerful. Kneeling above him, riding him to the pace I set, watching him writhe and groan underneath me as I slowly driving him out of his mind. Witnessing that pleasure overtake him, completely overwhelm him. Feeling him come apart in my arms because of what I'm doing to him.

And afterwards he was so sweet, so gentle, the way he kissed me, slow and tenderly, his emerald eyes staring deep into mine. I could see my own intense feelings reflected there, in his eyes. The expression of awestruck wonder on his face when he pulled me close and held me tight.

I sigh contentedly, snuggling closer. It's moments like these that make me want to stay here with him forever. I know my debt will be paid in a year, and after that he might not want anything more to do with me. But, it's hard to imagine, after making love with such sweet intensity, that he doesn't have some feelings for me as well. Maybe, in enough time, he will come to feel for me what I do for him.

He only has six more months in Ivan's employ. Just six more months. After that, maybe, just maybe, we could build a life together. It's possible…

Thinking about my debt brings my family to the forefront of my mind.

I wonder what Jeremy said to my mom about my choice to remain here with Dmitry? I try to imagine my mom's reaction when Jeremy tells her what I've done, but it's hard to picture when I don't even know where they are. Are they still in Pennsylvania? Are they even still in the country? They could be halfway around the world right now. Hell, for all I know, the Italians could have already hunted them down. They may be dead already, or kidnapped, or hurt somewhere…

Anxiety threatens to overwhelm me; there are too many unknowns.

"What's wrong?" Dmitry asks, pulling away slightly to look at me. He must feel the tension in my body.

"I was just wondering where you hid my mom and Jeremy."

"I can't tell you that," he answers. "It's safer for everyone if you don't know."

"I'm not going to say anything. They're my family! I would never put them at risk. I just want to know that they're all right."

"I told you they were. Do you not trust me?"

"What?" I ask, taken aback. Where did this come from? "Of course I trust you. I wouldn't be here if I didn't. But trusting you has nothing to do with wanting to know where my family is."

"You promised you'd stay here for a year." His voice takes on a hard edge, eyes frosting over. "Are you planning on running again?"

I sit up, pulling out of his embrace. "Is that what this is about? You think once I know where they are, I'll leave you? I told you I wouldn't run away again. Don't *you* trust *me*?"

The answer is in his eyes. No. He doesn't trust me. Even after I admitted I was wrong to leave, even though promised I wouldn't run again, he doesn't trust me to keep my word.

"They're my family!" I burst out angrily. "I should at least know where they are. At the very least, I should be able to contact them. Talk to them. Is that really so unreasonable a request?"

He studies me through narrowed eyes. "I can't tell you where they are. I know you would never intentionally give them up, but if you were somehow captured, it would be better for you if you don't know anything."

I open my mouth to argue further, but he raises a hand forestalling my arguments.

"But, if you want, you can call them once a week. More than that might draw unwanted attention to them, but once a week should be safe enough. That way you can know that they're okay, and that I'm not lying."

"It's not that I think you're lying," I say in exasperation. He looks so fierce, so guarded and offended. I never once implied that he was lying. Why would he be so quick to jump to that conclusion? "I just need to hear them for myself," I explain.

"Alright." He nods. "Tomorrow, after they've had time to settle in, you can call."

I sigh, relieved. "Thank you." I lean up and press a soft kiss to his lips. The stiffness in his features relaxes. Smiling to myself, I drape myself across his chest once more and drift off to sleep.

I wander the house anxiously the next day, waiting for Dmitry to finish with his meeting. I know I should be more upset that I'm basically being held prisoner here for the next year, even if I did agree to it. But if I'm honest with myself, it's a relief to not be home. To not deal with Ray, or worry about the rent payments, or go to my shitty waitressing job. All of the responsibility that normally weighs so heavily on my shoulders has been lifted.

Dmitry makes sure I have everything I need or could want—supplies for painting and drawing, books to read, food to eat. It's like a vacation. It's shocking to think that I'm actually happier here, in my captor's home, than I ever was living freely with my own family.

And the feelings I have developed for Dmitry are even more shocking. I try to remind myself that he's a criminal. That he's hurt people. That he's killed people. But when I look at him, all I see is the sweet, gentle, protective man who's been taking care of me, whose clever hands and mouth can stroke my body into such ecstasy.

Images from last night flash through my mind, heating my skin and sending zing's of arousal through my body. I shift uncomfortably.

To distract myself, I begin unpacking the bag that Viktor brought, placing the meager collection of clothes neatly into the dresser drawers in the spare room.

When I first packed this bag, I thought I'd only be gone a week. Now that I'm going to be here for at least a year, I'll need to make a trip back to my house and grab the rest of my clothing. If the Italians haven't already staked the house out by now, that is.

My thoughts are so occupied with this latest problem that at first I don't register what the small packet in my hand is. When it does register, I gasp, pack of pills dropping on the floor, hands covering my mouth.

Oh, my God! My birth control pills! I completely forgot about them! I started taking it a couple years ago, but I've never been very good at remembering to take it every day. I've only been using them to help regulate my cycle—it's not like I've needed them for any other reason. Not until recently…

I quickly do the math in my head, and feel my stomach pinch. The last time I took it was Friday. Today is Wednesday. I've been without my pills for nearly a week.

Oh, shit…

No. No, I can't be pregnant. It's only been a few days. I can't possibly be pregnant.

I open the circular lid and let out a whimper as I see precisely half the pills missing. I'm smack in the middle of my cycle. Fuck.

Dizziness overwhelms me. I sway, blindly reaching for the bed to lower myself onto. It can't be. It would be a cruel joke of the universe if I were to get pregnant the first time I have sex. My luck can't possibly be that bad.

I sit there, staring into space, fighting off a mild panic attack, when suddenly the image of a tiny infant with bright green eyes pops into my mind, unbidden. A perfect little baby boy with Dmitry's beautiful eyes.

I feel my heart squeeze. But then I imagine Dmitry's horrified expression when I tell him I'm carrying his child. And he *would* be horrified, wouldn't he? I mean, I'm just some woman he purchased at a sex auction. One of many he's bought over the years, I imagine. He wouldn't want a child with me.

The squealing of tires out front snaps me out of my whirling thoughts. Fear pulses through me, swift and strong. I run into the living room in time to see headlights burst through the window, blinding me. A horn honks once, twice, three times, then a deep male voice yells my name.

Oh God, have the Italians found me already?

I dart to the desk and fumble around for the gun Dmitry put there yesterday. It's clumsy in my hands, the smooth handle nearly slipping right out of my sweat-dampened palms.

"Open up, Daisy!" A heavy hand bangs on the front door, rattling in on its hinges.

How the hell do I use this thing? It is even loaded? God, why didn't I let Dmitry show me how to use it yesterday? What a stubborn idiot I can be sometimes!

With my heart pounding out of my chest, I approach the door cautiously. I jump when the man behind it bangs on it again. "God dammit," I hear him mutter. "Open the fucking door!"

I peek out the peephole and gasp. I don't recognize the tall, blond man outside, but the man hanging limply at his side is all too familiar, even covered in blood the way he is.

Dmitry's hair hangs into his face, his eyes closed, lips slightly parted on a groan of pain. The whole of his white linen shirt is stained crimson, a shade so bright it's startling. Make-shift bandages are wrapped around his chest and torso, but they've already been soaked through. The sheer amount of blood covering him sends me into a near panic, but I beat it back.

I throw the door open and point the barrel of the gun at the stranger's face. He freezes in shock, one hand raised to pound on the door again.

"What did you do to him?" My hands shake, but my voice is somehow steady. It doesn't sound like my own voice. It's low, dangerous. My legs tremble and my stomach pitches sickeningly, but underneath the fear and worry is a rage unlike anything I've ever felt. My finger twitches on the trigger. I have no idea if the gun is even loaded or how to use it, but standing this close to my target, I assume all I have to do is pull the trigger and this man will die.

"Whoa, whoa! Calm down! I didn't do this! We were ambushed at the meeting. It wasn't me!"

"Who the hell are you?" I ask, hands still shaking. The blond man holds up one arm—the one that's not supporting Dmitry—as if to show me he isn't armed.

"Nice to finally meet you in person, Daisy," he says. "Though I wish it was under better circumstances. I'm Josef. I work with Dmitry."

He works with him in the Russian Mob. Jesus, is he a hitman too? Rather than ask that, I ask instead, "What happened to him? Is he going to be okay?"

"I didn't hurt him, I swear. He's my friend. I'm trying to help him. And if you want him to survive, you need to get the hell out of the way."

Slowly, I lower the gun and move to the side. Josef carries Dmitry to the kitchen table and lays him down on it.

"Shouldn't you put him on the couch or something?" I ask.

"Gotta get the bullets out first," he says without looking at me. He produces a terrifyingly large knife from a sheath on his belt and sets to work cutting Dmitry's bandages and clothes off. I gasp as his broad chest is revealed. There are two small puncture wounds, one next to his right shoulder, the other lower down and to the left. Despite the small size of the holes, the amount of blood still oozing out of them is terrifying.

"Oh, my God! Is he going to be okay?"

"If I can get the bullets out," he says as he examines the wounds with a critical eye. "It doesn't look like anything vital was pierced, thank God."

"What happened?"

"The Italians showed up at the meeting and tried to kill the boss. Dmitry, dumb shit that he is, dove in front of Ivan and took a bullet for his trouble."

My breath catches in my lungs. *My God...*

"Shouldn't you take him to a hospital or something?" Before the words even leave my mouth, I realize how stupid they are. Dmitry and Josef are in the Russian mob. Of course they can't go to the hospital. "Or, like, a doctor. You guys have that, don't you? Doctors who work for your...organization?"

"Yeah, but he's out of town. So for now, it looks like I'm your man. And I'm going to need your help getting these bullets out."

Josef disappears into the bathroom, returning with a bag full of medical instruments. He pulls out a pair of scary looking pincers and gives me a look that chills my blood.

"You're going to have to hold him still. This is going to hurt."

Swallowing my fear, I reach for Dmitry's broad shoulders and pin them to the table as hard as I can.

Josef takes a breath, then inserts the pincers into the wound at Dmitry's shoulder. Dmitry comes to on scream.

My eyes tear up at the pain in his voice, but I keep hold of him as Josef continues digging around, searching for the bullet.

The next hour is harrowing. After that first scream, Dmitry stays silent as Josef works on him. Josef shows no mercy as he relentlessly digs out not just the two bullets, but several pieces of fabric from Dmitry's shirt as well.

By the time he finishes, Dmitry is as white as a sheet and on the verge of passing out again. I've mostly held myself together up until now, focusing solely on what needs to be done and not thinking too much about what could have happened to Dmitry. What could still happen.

People die of gunshot wounds all the time, and that's when they're treated in a sterile hospital. The environment Josef is forced to work in right now is far from sterile. Dmitry could get an infection, or Josef could have missed a nick in a major organ. Josef doesn't have any formal medical training, at least none that he's mentioned. He could so easily miss something. By the time the symptoms of a potential complication show up, it might be too late.

Finally, hours later, Josef sews up the last stitch and sags back in exhaustion. His hands and arms are coated in dried blood, and I can't keep back my tears any longer. They come in a torrent, tears spilling down my cheeks, breath rasping in and out in great heaves as I stare down at the mess of Dmitry's beautiful skin.

He's already been marked in so many ways, and now there are two more scars added to the mix of pain and anguish. And these two scars might be the death of him yet. Just because they're stitched up and no longer leaking blood doesn't mean that Dmitry will recover. So many things could still go wrong...

I'm so lost in my grief, sobbing uncontrollably, that I jump when a warm hand caresses my cheek. I open my eyes to see Dmitry's emerald gaze on mine, his thumb wiping away my tears as they fall.

"It's okay, baby. It's going to be okay."

"I thought you were dead. When we dragged you in here, I thought you were dead." I collapse onto his chest, dissolving into tears again. His hand brushes through my hair in a calming rhythm, soothing me until I'm all cried out.

When I'm finally empty of tears, I raise my head to find Josef is gone. Dmitry is looking up at me with a strange expression on his face, a mixture between tenderness and confusion. Sitting up, I wipe my cheeks with the backs of my hands. I clear my throat and try to pull myself together. But when I look down at Dmitry's chest again and see those freshly stitched up wounds again, my eyes tear up.

"He didn't even cover the wound," I say, my voice rough with tears and burning with indignation. "They could get infected. What was he thinking?"

I fumble around in the medical kit Josef left, looking for some bandages. Dmitry places a hand on my arm, stopping my frantic search. I realize I'm trembling.

"Daisy," he says. "It really is going to be okay. They didn't hit anything major. The wounds are superficial at best."

"Superficial wounds?" I say, "You call this a superficial wound? Dmitry, you could have *died*. Hell, you still can! You could get an infection, or Josef could have missed something, or...or..." I gasp in a breath, fighting to find the words. "These are NOT superficial wounds!" I finally say, slamming the medical kit onto the table.

Dmitry gives me that look again, the one of tenderness and bewilderment.

"You're not in any danger," he says, still watching me curiously. "They were after Ivan. They won't come here."

"You think that's what I'm worried about right now? God, Dmitry, I'm worried about *you!* You could have died. Don't you get that? Don't you understand that—" I freeze midsentence and snap my mouth shut. Crap, did I almost just say that?

"Understand what?"

"Nothing. It's nothing." I turn away, pretending to look for more bandages as my cheeks flood with heat.

Dmitry grabs my arm and forces me to face him.

"Tell me." His emerald eyes burn with intensity. He isn't going to let me go until I answer him. And looking at him now, I realize there really isn't any point in keeping it to myself any longer. It's too late for that.

I take a deep breath, steadying myself, and meet his gaze squarely.

"I love you, Dmitry. I love you, and you could have died tonight. You *would* have died, if Josef hadn't brought you here and patched you up. God, when I think about what could have happened, how close you were… I've never seen so much blood before in my life. I really thought you were going to die, and you would never have known how I feel about you. I love you, Dmitry. I'm in love with you."

I look down at the floor, my cheeks ablaze. As the silence drags on, my humiliation grows. When he finally does speak, it's almost worse than if he had stayed quiet.

"You're in love with me?" He sounds floored, as if he can't possibly believe I just said that.

"I know you only bought me at the auction for…" I stumble over the words 'for sex'. "I know you don't feel the same way," I amend. "And that's fine. I'm not asking you for anything. I just needed you to know." I twist my fingers together over and over again, squirming under the thick tension filling the air between us.

His rough voice finally breaks the silence. "Daisy, look at me."

I squeeze my hands together and square my jaw, gathering my courage. Strong fingers lift my chin until I'm gazing into Dmitry's intense eyes.

I lose myself in those eyes. The rest of the world fades away, and it's just me and Dmitry. I forget all about the Italians or my family, or Josef off somewhere in the house. All that matters is Dmitry here in front of me, warm and alive and *mine*.

He reaches a hand out to cup my cheek and pulls me to him. His mouth crushes mine in a hard, possessive kiss. His tongue invades my mouth, plundering it as if feasting on an exquisite desert he just can't get enough of.

After a few minutes, we're both panting hard. A sheen of sweat has formed on his brow, but he's still staring at me as if he wants to devour me.

"Now, now," an amused voice interrupts. "Enough of that. You're barely stitched up as it is." Josef casually strolls into the room, a sly smile stretching his lips. "Let me wrap up those wounds and then I'll be out of your hair."

I laugh shakily and step back to give Josef room to work.

Good thing he interrupted when he did, or who knows what he would have walked in on…

Josef winks at me as if reading my thoughts, causing my cheeks to heat even more.

Dmitry growls, glaring at him as is he wants to run him through, but he doesn't protest as Josef starts swiping his chest with Iodine and covering his wounds with gauze.

When Josef finally finishes, he helps me carry Dmitry to bed. Despite Dmitry's best efforts, his eyes begin to sag as exhaustion overtakes him. He's asleep before Josef even leaves the room. I walk him to the front door.

"Well, Daisy, I've heard so much about you. It was nice to finally meet you in person."

"Sorry, but I can't say the same about you," I respond. As much as I appreciate Josef helping Dmitry tonight, there's something unsettling about him, keeping me on edge. His smiles, though frequent, never reach his eyes, and there's a dangerous, predatory air about him that has all my senses on high alert.

He smiles wider, sensing my discomfort. "You don't scare easily do you?"

I don't answer. I just open the door for him, hoping he'll take the hint and leave. No such luck.

"You're good for him, you know that?" He crosses his arms and leans back against the doorjamb as if settling in for a nice, long chat.

"What do you mean?" I ask, unable to contain my curiosity.

As uncomfortable as he makes me, I can't ignore the fact that he has known Dmitry much longer than I have. The desire to know more about Dmitry's life gnaws at me.

"I'm just another virgin he bought at the auction," I continue, humiliation still a scorched wound inside my chest. It didn't slip my notice that when I told Dmitry I loved him, he didn't say anything back.

"Just another virgin?" Josef says, eyebrows raised in disbelief. "What, you think Dmitry goes to those auctions and buys girls regularly?"

"Well, doesn't he?"

Josef laughs. He throws his head back and laughs as if this is the funniest thing he's ever heard.

"Dmitry?" He laughs even harder, wiping his eyes. "Dmitry hasn't been with a woman in I don't know how long. Hell, I'm not sure he's *ever* been with one. And if he has, he sure as shit never talked about her."

"Then why did he bid on me if he's never done that before?"

"Well, sweetheart, that's a question you're going to have to ask him. 'Night," he says with cheery wave, disappearing down the dark driveway.

Dmitry remains asleep for the rest of the night and well into the next morning. I spend the long night by his bedside, routinely checking for any signs of fever or infection. I don't even change my clothes for fear that the moment I turn my back, he'll flare up with a fever or go into cardiac arrest.

Thankfully, his skin stays cool and no redness or puffiness develops near the bullet wounds. I try not to think too much, but despite my best efforts, my mind wanders back through the years, to memories of my mom and her long list of men.

I can't count the number of times my mom's boyfriends have come home hurt or beaten after a drunken stupor or deal gone wrong. The amount of times my mom cried her eyes out and sat by their bedside all night, taking care of their bloody, stinking mess.

And that's exactly what I'm doing now.

Here I am, sitting by Dmitry's bed, hoping and praying it will be alright, when I know it never will. How could it, when this is what he does for a living? He's an enforcer. He worked for the Russian Mafia for Christ's sake. This is all just a normal day for him.

Is this what I've become? Is this how my mom felt with every loser boyfriend of hers? Love and fear and anger, all at once while praying and hoping that somehow he'll miraculously change? I've seen it too many times. I know men don't change. So how can I still have hope that Dmitry will? He's said he wanted to get out. He said he had a plan. Just six more months. Can I handle six more months of this? Six more months of gut-wrenching fear every time he leaves the house? This nauseating worry that any day could be his last?

Chapter 23

DMITRY

"Hey." My voice sounds rougher than usual. She jumps, startled, her sleep-hazed eyes finding mine. She leaps up as if coming out of a trance and grabs a vial of pills and a glass of water from the table.

"Here, take these," she says. "They'll help with the pain."

She puts an arm around my back and helps me sit up. Fire engulfs my chest and side, but I clench my jaw and don't make a sound. She looks freaked out enough as it is. I don't want to scare her any more than I already have.

I take the pills and swallow them dry, not even looking to see what they are. The instinctive trust this implies startles me. In the sort of life I lived, trust is a rare commodity. Even among friends, trust is rare. If it were anyone else, I would have checked the pills, or refused them completely for fear that they may be laced. It's not uncommon for rival gangs to drug you to get information or poison you entirely to take out the competition.

"Have you been up all night?" I ask her, noticing her messy hair and blood-stained clothes.

She avoids my gaze when she answers. "I just wanted to make sure you were okay." Her cheeks turn pink with embarrassment and I'm reminded of her confession yesterday.

She said she loves me.

My chest pulls tight at the memory. She loves me? How can that be? I've all but abducted her and forced her into my bed. How the hell can she love me?

Because she doesn't know the truth, a dark voice whispers inside. She doesn't know the true depths of my deceit. If she was privy to the darkest parts of my soul, aware of my twisted obsession with her, the number of nights I've watched her through her bedroom window, stalked her back and forth from work, or the twisted methods I used to trap her here with me, she'd despise me. Absolutely and completely.

I know I don't deserve someone like her. Someone so selfless and kind and strong and beautiful. But, for the first time in my life, I wish that I did. I wish I could be who she sees when she looks at me with such trust and openness. For the first time, I wish that I could deserve that trust. That I could earn it, somehow. Maybe it's too late. Maybe the crimes I've committed against her and so many others in my life are already too great, but I have to try. I have to somehow be worthy of the trust and love she's gifting me with.

"I'm okay, Daisy," I say, needing to erase the worry shadowing her beautiful eyes. I reach out and gently brush her tear-stained cheek. With gentle pressure, I turn her to face me, forcing her to meet my eyes. "I really am. You don't need to worry about anything."

Tears spring to her eyes, a mixture of fear and outrage shining in them. "Don't need to worry? Dmitry, you almost died! How can I not worry? Every time you're out there, working for those people, your life is in danger. How am I going to 'not worry' every time you leave the house? Every time you go to work? I mean, how often does this sort of thing happen? Are you routinely gunned down like this? Is this all just a normal part of working for the mob?"

I've never seen her so upset. So angry. Not many men are brave enough to stand up to me, or even raise their voice to me. Yet here is this little slip of a thing, quivering with rage, hands balled into fists, shouting at me. I try to fight it back, but a smile pulls at my lips. She isn't afraid of me. That thought alone makes the pain from the gunshots fade better than any of the drugs on the market.

"No," I say, still fighting a smile. "This doesn't happen often. Tonight was unusual. In all the years I've worked for Ivan, I've only been shot three times."

Rather than put her at ease, her eyes widen in fear. "Where? What happened? Are you okay?"

"I'm fine," I reassure her. "I healed, just like I'll heal this time. These wounds aren't even that serious. I'll be up and moving in a day. What I'm more concerned about is how they knew where we were."

"What do you mean?"

"It's like they knew exactly where we were meeting. Ivan's usually so careful, especially now with the Italians trying to make a push into our territory. Most of us don't even know when the meeting will take place until thirty minutes beforehand. Only those closest to Ivan have any advanced warning. I just don't know how the Italians got there so fast."

She looks at me sharply. "You think one of the Russians told them?"

I shake my head. "No. They're all loyal to Ivan. None of them have any reason to double cross him." But even as I say this, my mind turns the problem over. If there were a traitor, it would explain why I've yet to find Freddy's partner. But it doesn't make any sense. The only people who could have tipped off the Italians early enough were those in Ivan's inner circle, and I can't imagine any of them turning on him. I've worked with them since I was a boy. They are all loyal to the grave.

"So what are you going to do?" she asks, fear still in her eyes.

Shoving these troubling questions to the back of my mind, I give her a crooked smile. "First, I'm going to teach you how to shoot."

Chapter 24

DAISY

I fight him at first, but eventually give in. He's relentless, insisting that I need to learn to protect myself. But it's not myself I want to protect. Despite his repeated assurances that he'd be back to normal within a day, I see the stiff way he's moving, how slowly even the simplest tasks are for him. If the Italians come to the house now, Dmitry is a dead man.

So I give in. If the Italians come to finish him off, they won't be leaving unscathed.

He starts slowly, at first just familiarizing me with the basic mechanics of a handgun. He teaches me how to load and unload it, how to clean it, even how to take it completely apart and put it back to together.

Once Dmitry is able to move around more easily, he takes me outside for target practice. Actually firing the gun is terrifying, but exhilarating at the same time. To feel that kind of power in your hands: literally the power of life and death. I think the part that scares me the most is how much I like it. And Dmitry's beaming grin as I become more and more proficient is even better than the shooting. After a couple weeks, I'm able to hit the target more than fifty percent of the time.

But, all too soon, time passes and Dmitry recovers enough to go back to work. All the relief I've felt as he slowly recovered evaporates. Today, he'll be back out there, with those people, possibly getting shot again.

"Do you really have to go back today?" I study his face, searching for any sign of lingering pain, any possible reason I can come up with to convince him to stay home another few days.

Despite his injuries, these past few weeks have been incredible. Dmitry has been more open since his injury, less guarded with me than before. He's smiled and laughed more in these weeks than I thought he was capable of. I've gotten to know the real Dmitry that hides behind the scary mobster persona he shows the rest of the world. And even though I know he might end up breaking my heart, I've only fallen more in love with him.

The thought of him leaving today, of what could happen to him, has me in a near panic. I try to hide it, but the way his gaze softens as he scrutinizes my face, I know he sees it nonetheless.

"Everything will be fine. I promise. The sooner I finish up these last months with them, the sooner I'll be out. I'll be finished with all of this, and then you and I can leave. We can get your family and leave here, go wherever you want. I just need to finish up this last bit of business."

My chest warms, heart swelling. He hasn't said he loves me. He's never reciprocated after my embarrassing confession the night he was shot. But the very fact that he's talking about his future plans as if I'm a part of them, too, shows he at least feels something for me. It's true that we made a deal for me to stay for a year, but he's talking as if he plans on keeping me with him longer than that. He's talking as if he plans on turning this into forever.

Despite my fears, I smile back at him, already envisioning us living on a beach somewhere far away from all of this. I could paint and he could carve. My mom can finally live an easy life instead of working herself to death. Maybe, with a little peace and quiet to discover what he wants to do with his life, my brother might even mature a bit and learn how to take care of himself.

The fantasy gives me the courage I need to let him leave, rather than begging him to stay and hide with me instead.

"Yeah, I know. Just…be careful, okay?" I respond.

He leans down and brushes my lips with his. "I promise."

Taking a deep breath, I gather my courage. "I love you," I say. "You don't have to say anything back," I hurry to reassure him. "I just needed to say it, before you go. You know, in case anything happens." I haven't said those words since that horrific night, but I couldn't bear the thought of letting him leave now without telling him again.

He gives me a boyish, lopsided grin. "Daisy," he says softly. "I love you too."

My breath catches in my throat. He said it. He actually said it. He loves me.

Joy unlike anything I've ever known explodes inside of me. I leap up, wrapping my arms around him, kissing him for all I'm worth. He kisses me back just as fiercely, our lips and tongues and teeth clashing together in a primal dance of dominance and possession. His hands tear at my clothes, stripping me bare in a matter of seconds. He lays me down right there, on the floor of the entrance way.

Rasping heated words of love and desire in my ear, his body possesses mine. He isn't gentle; neither of us is. My nails rake his back while he thrusts furiously inside me, claiming me, body and soul. But he doesn't complain, and his injuries don't seem to slow him down at all. Any doubts I have about him being fully healed vanish.

All too soon, it's over and he's getting dressed again. I stand there, naked and exposed, fighting the urge to drag him into the bedroom with me, never letting him go.

His gaze meets mine, and he pulls me back to him for one more kiss. Neither of us wants to let go, but we know he must. Before he leaves, he hands me the small pistol he usually keeps in the desk drawer.

"Promise me you'll keep this on you. And don't open the door. Not for anyone, do you understand? Now that the Italians failed to kill Ivan, they'll be even more dangerous. They tipped their hand, and they know it's only a matter of time before we come for them."

I nod, taking the small gun into my hand. Since learning how to actually use it, I'm no longer afraid of it, but I still don't know whether I'll have the courage to actually use it if the time comes. I don't know if I'd be able to shoot another human being, regardless of the threat they pose. But I nod anyway and try to look brave. Dmitry has enough on his plate right now. The last thing he needs is to worry about me while I'm safe at home.

He kisses me one last time, then he's gone, and I'm left with nothing to do but wander listlessly around the empty house, worrying and praying that he'll make it home safe tonight.

I cook and clean, scrubbing every inch of the house until the floors sparkle and the windows shine, but it does little to distract me from my worry. When I run out of things to do in the house, I head into the backyard, intent on exhausting myself with some yard work. The garden bordering the back of the house is a bit overgrown, so I search the shed that doubles as Dmitry's workshop for some garden tools.

I take a moment to appreciate his carvings all around. A large one captures my eye, one I haven't seen before. It's me. Just my head and upper torso, but it's life-size. In fact, I lean up close to it and realize it's almost the exact same size as myself, and so exquisitely done, every detail perfect. I wonder how long it took him to make this. I've only been here a few weeks, but the level of detail in this piece looks as if it would have taken months.

I tear my gaze from the impressive work and look around for the garden tools. The statue sits on a large wooden desk, so I search the drawers, hoping to find a small weeding claw or even some gloves. But I don't find either of those things. Instead, I find a stack of photographs.

With shaking hands, I reach out and pick the first one up for a closer inspection. The picture is grainy, as if taken in low light from some distance away. I recognize myself in an instant, the ugly yellow uniform I'm wearing only too familiar. But Dmitry has never seen me in that uniform. I haven't been to work since before the auction. I've most definitely been fired by now since I haven't shown up for any of my shifts. When was this taken? How did he get it?

I slowly flip through the stack, my stomach tightening sickeningly as I scan picture after picture. Dozens of images, all of me. Me, working at the diner. Laughing in my living room with my brother. Glaring at Ray outside of our home. Crying alone in my bedroom.

How did he get these? When?

None of the pictures are time stamped. There's no way to tell how long he's been watching me. Stalking me. But how? Why? And how is it that he just happened to be at the auction the night I was up for sale? Josef said himself he's never known Dmitry to buy women there. So why me?

The hair on the back of my neck prickles in warning. A moment later, there's a sound behind me. I spin around, but I'm too late. A hand covers my mouth before I can get out a scream. I kick and thrash, but the man holding me just tightens his grip.

He lifts me easily and drags me from the shed, shoving a dark cloth over my eyes, blocking my sight. A gag replaces the hand on my mouth. I shriek into the cloth, but it's no use. There's no one around for miles, and Dmitry isn't due back until later tonight. My hand goes to the holster on my ankle, but it's empty. I remember, too late, that I left the gun inside on the table. I didn't feel comfortable carrying it on me while I mopped and cleaned. And, despite Dmitry getting shot a couple weeks ago, I never truly believed I would be in any danger. Not here. Dmitry's cabin has always seemed so safe, so secluded.

But that illusion of safety has been shattered. The seclusion works against me now; there's no one around to hear me scream or see these men drag me from the shed and shove me into the back of a vehicle.

They're going to kill me. Dmitry warned me to keep the gun on me, but I didn't listen, and now I'm going to die. I can only hope they'll do it fast. I pray that they'll kill me before Dmitry finds us. I can't let them torture me in front of him the way they did his family. Please, don't let him relive that horror because of me.

Chapter 25

DMITRY

I shift in the uncomfortable seat, cursing myself for insisting on going back to work today. The wounds in my chest and side hurt more than I let on, the burn and deep ache telling me I'm a far way from being fully healed. I should have taken an extra week or two off. No one would have argued. Not after I got shot saving Ivan's life. Ivan himself tried to insist I rest longer. But no, like a dumb ass, I insisted on getting back to work.

I need to find the fuckers that shot me. I need to find out how those scum bags knew exactly where and when that meeting was. I dismissed Daisy's inside job theory when she first said it, but after running it over and over in my head, I'm not as sure. There have been a lot of coincidences lately, things that could only be explained if *someone* was feeding them information. If one of our men is working with the Italians, I need to know who. Until I do, Daisy won't be safe.

So instead of spending the morning in bed with Daisy, I'm sweating and uncomfortable in this car, staking out a restaurant known to be frequented by members of the Moreno organization. What the fuck was I thinking?

My phone rings. I curse as I reach for it, the movement pulling at my barely healed shoulder.

"Dmitry," I answer.

"We have your girl." The voice is smooth and calm with a slight hint of an Italian accent.

The air rushes from my lungs, the whole world narrowing down to a tiny pinprick.

"Who is this?" I growl into the phone.

"Be at Antonelli's in thirty minutes. Come alone and unarmed, or the girl dies."

"If you fucking hurt her—"

The phone cuts out before I finish my threat.

"FUCK!" I slam my fist into the steering wheel, ignoring the burn in my shoulder. They're dead. The entire Italian mob will die for touching her.

The restaurant he specified is across town. I have to speed to get there in time. I drive like a man possessed, running red lights and weaving through the midday traffic. Horns blare behind me, but they barely register. All I can think is, *Daisy's going to die because of me.*

I knew I'd end up getting her killed. Just like I got my mom and sister killed. I'm tainted. Cursed. What was I thinking, involving someone as innocent as her in my hellhole of a life?

I pound my fist on the steering wheel again, as angry with myself as with the men who took her. If they hurt her, I will kill them all.

Tires squeal as I come to a stop in front of Antonelli's. I shove my gun in my glove box before rushing through the front doors. They'd be idiotic not to search me and I'd rather not lose my favorite piece. But if they think lack of a weapon will save them from me, they are sorely mistaken. I don't need a gun to kill them; I'll snap their fucking necks with my bare hands.

"Where is she?" I snarl at the first man I see. He blanches at my expression. These fuckers have no idea who they're dealing with. There's a reason my own men call me the Beast. I will tear them limb from limb and dance in a shower of their blood.

"They're - they're downstairs," he stutters, backing away from the murder in my eyes.

Shoving him out of my way, I head down the stairs, forcing myself to slow my pace, evaluate the situation. An icy calm settles over me, the same calm I call forth whenever I'm on a hit. My mind clears, allowing me to focus on the problem at hand.

The hallway at the bottom of the stairs is overflowing with Italians. All of them are armed and alert, watching me warily as I stalk past them. At the end of the narrow passage, two large bodyguards bar the door. Daisy must be behind there.

I force myself to remain still while the men frisk me, searching for any hidden weapons. When they're satisfied, they move aside, allowing me to enter the room.

My eyes immediately go to Daisy. She's bound and gagged, tied to a chair against the far wall. Despite the fear I see on her face, her jaw is clenched tight, teeth bared like a feral animal while she stares down Nicholas, the head of the Italian Mafia. When she sees me, her whole body jerks in my direction. She fights against the ropes, yelling something unintelligible through the gag. The fear in her face becomes even more pronounced when the two burly men close and lock the door behind me.

"Untie her," I say to Nicholas, my voice low and dangerous.

"You're not in a position to make demands," sneers Nicky, Nicholas's idiot son. He reminds me of Viktor, the way he wears his arrogance like a shield, too stupid to realize how vulnerable he truly is. He stands behind his father's chair, chin raised haughtily.

Cute. He thinks he actually has the upper hand here. Without moving my eyes from his, I count five men in here, including Nicholas and Nicky. Fucking child's play. Even without my weapons, I know I can take them out before they land a fatal shot on me.

As if recognizing this, Nicholas makes a motion with his head. One of the large bodyguards steps closer to Daisy. If anything happens to them, her life will be forfeit. Maybe he isn't as stupid as he looks.

"Shut up, Nicky," Nicholas says, shooting a chastising look over his shoulder. Nicky's eyes flash in anger, but after a moment, he lowers his gaze. Once Nicholas is looking at me again Nicky shoots me a threatening glare, as if it's my fault he was reprimanded.

"Relax, Dmitry," he says to me. "I have no intention of harming your woman, so long as you don't force my hand. Now, we seem to have a bit of a situation between our families. I've invited you here so we can discuss how we can settle this."

"A 'situation?'" I say, letting my sarcasm leak into my tone. "You mean when you tried to kill Ivan? Is that what you mean by a 'situation'?"

"Yes, I heard there was an incident last week at one of his clubs. But I can assure you, I didn't order any hit."

Nicholas leans back in his chair, the picture of ease. Behind him, Nicky shifts and looks away.

"We want to make sure there won't be any retaliation" Nicholas continues. "After all, we didn't retaliate when you killed our man, Freddy."

"He stole money from us."

"Which is why I looked the other way. I have no desire to war with Ivan. We've worked well together these last years. Let's not do anything to upset that balance, shall we?"

I stare him down, not responding,

"It's not as if there was any lasting damage. Ivan survived, after all, so no harm done."

Daisy begins thrashing against her bonds again. She manages to push the gag out of her mouth and starts yelling at Nicholas. "No harm? No harm?! You shot Dmitry! You almost killed him!"

Nicholas motions with his head and one of the bodyguards step forward to put the gag back in.

"Don't fucking touch her," I warn him.

He hesitates, then takes another step toward her.

I lash out, my fist colliding with his face before he reaches his holster. He drops to the ground with a roar, his hands covering his broken nose, blood already leaking from between his fingers.

The rest of the room draws their weapons, but I've already stepped back, hands out to show them I'm finished.

"I told him not to touch her."

Anger sparks in Nicholas' eyes, but he suppresses it.

"Fine, fine, leave it off," he says with a wave of his hand. "I had heard that you were injured in that unfortunate incident, but you have clearly made a full recovery."

Daisy opens her mouth to yell again, but subsides at the look I give her.

"So, you're proposing a truce, then? Between you and Ivan?"

"Exactly. As I said before, I didn't order the hit. Believe me, Ivan and I may have our differences, but none of us wants a war. War cuts into profits. You promise me there will be no retaliatory action on his part, and I will let your girl here live."

"You know I can't speak for Ivan."

"But you can influence him. He listens to you. Convince him to let this go."

"Otherwise," Nicky chimes in, "We'll have to come back for little Daisy here. Maybe we'll give her some marks to match your own, huh?"

Rage flashes through me like wildfire. He all but admitted that they're the ones responsible for killing my family and carving me up.

"Touch her and I'll fucking kill you."

"I have to say, I'm surprised you're so concerned about her welfare, considering you're the reason she's in this predicament," he says with a sneer.

Panic spikes in my chest, but I don't allow any of it to show on my face. He can't possibly know.

Nicholas watches on curiously, but doesn't interfere.

Daisy looks outraged at first, then confused. She glances back and forth between us, as if she's not sure she heard him right. "What are you talking about?"

"Oh, didn't you know?" Nicky asks, eyes glinting spitefully. "Dmitry here is the one who tricked your step-daddy out of all that money. He's the reason you were at that auction at begin with."

Shock rushes through me, and Nicky sees it before I can hide it. "Yeah, I know all about that. It's the only possible explanation as to why a beauty like her would be with a beast like you."

"Dmitry?" Daisy says, her innocent eyes on me, pleading for me to deny it.

"Oh no, I guess she didn't know. Oh, well. These things never stay a secret for long."

"You can untie her now," Nicholas says, nodding to the guard nearest her whose broken nose is still oozing blood. The guard glares at me, both eyes already darkening.

"I trust you can convince Ivan to see reason on this matter. If not, well… you know what the consequences will be."

With equal parts rage and dread, I tuck daisy under my arm to lead her out. She pushes me away, eyes glaring at me in betrayal. Her rejection stings, but it's no less than I deserve.

"We need to get out of here," I whisper low enough so only she can hear. "We'll talk about it later."

Her eyes spit fire at me, but she allows me to lead her from the room.

Chapter 26

DAISY

I'm numb as he drags me out of the restaurant. What does this all mean?

As soon as we're at his car, I yank my arm away from him. I can't stand to have him touch me right now. The lies, the deceit. God, he's made such a fool of me.

As he pulls away from the curb, I turn to him, rage and disbelief bursting from inside me.

"What did he mean, Dmitry? What was he talking about?" But I know. Even as I ask these questions, I know the answer. Dmitry did this. Somehow, he is responsible for my family's debt, for the auction, for everything. It all starts to make sense.

"The photos. The bath products. Ray's sudden, inexplicable debt when he's never been much of a gambler. And you. You just happened to show up at that auction, even though Josef says you've never bought a girl from one before. You planned all this.

You've been spying on me and you planned this entire thing, right down to the art supplies and what conditioner I use!"

He doesn't deny it. His jaw clenches, his hands tightening on the steering wheel.

All this time, I thought he was protecting me, when he was the one who was putting me in danger. The betrayal of it cuts deep.

"You plunged my family into debt, forced me to sell my body like a whore, then bought me to use for yourself? Do you know how fucked up that is? What the hell is wrong with you? What gives you the right to mess with my life like that? To trap me in your twisted games and keep me prisoner?"

Then a horrible thought occurs to me.

"Oh my God—my brother's debt. Did you orchestrate that too? Did you involve my brother in your sick plans?"

"No, I had nothing to do with that. I only heard about it from Viktor the day before Jeremy showed up to take you. Viktor planned to use that debt to force you into his bed."

"Oh, the way you did?"

"I never forced you into my bed. My house, yes, but never my bed. You came to that willingly. And Ray is the one who ran you into debt. He may not be big on gambling, but he is an addict. All I had to do was have Josef hike up the price of the smack he was selling him, then make a few mentions of some games nearby where he could make enough to feed his addiction. Yeah, I had Josef encourage him to borrow more money, but the decision was Ray's. He could have stopped at any point, but he didn't. It was only a matter of time before he cashed a check you couldn't pay. It's the same thing my dad did. An addict will always put his family in danger. At least my plan kept you out of the hands of the true sickos who frequent those auctions."

"Is that why you chose me? I reminded you of the sister and mom you couldn't save, so you set out to 'save' me instead? You forced me to sell myself so you could buy me? Why me? Why do you have all those pictures of me in your shed?" I ask in a shaky voice. "How long have you been watching me? How long have you been planning this?"

He unlocks his jaw and glances at me before continuing to stare ahead at the road.

"Six months," he finally says.

My jaw drops. "Six months?" It's inconceivable. He's been stalking me for half a year. Following me, watching me, taking *pictures* of me… *What the fuck?*

"Why me? Out of everyone you could have chosen, why did you do this to *me*?" My voice breaks on the last word. To think that he planned this all out, that he purposely set out to ruin my life… My stomach pitches. I think I'm going to be sick…

"I saw you at the diner one night. You were just getting ready to leave. I heard you laughing with that other waitress, the one with the red hair. There was just something about you. You were so… innocent. So light and free. Open. Your eyes were sparkling as you teased her about some guy she was dating. I had had a bad night. Doing what I do, I have a lot of bad nights. But just sitting there listening to you joke and laugh behind the counter with her… I can't explain it, but it made me relax for the first time in a long time.

"I followed you home that night," he admits. "Didn't even stay to eat. You left out the back door, and I didn't even think about it. I was up and out of the door before I realized what I was doing. I stayed behind you the whole walk home, sticking to the shadows. You never noticed me, never turned around. When I saw you enter your house, I couldn't help myself. I sat outside and watched you move from room to room. I watched you tidy up the house and kitchen, even though it was well past midnight. Then you went into your room to shower. I almost left then, almost walked away, but when you came back you sat down, your wet hair pulled into a knot high on your head, and started drawing on that big easel in your room.

"The look on your face while you sketched… It was like all the bad shit in the world just disappeared. You were so at peace. So sweet and innocent and content. I stood out there in the freezing cold and watched you for hours before you finally went to sleep."

"I left then, and went home. In my line of work, all the stress and blood and shit, it gets to you. I hadn't slept longer than a few hours at a time in months, but after I watched you, for the first time in a long time, I was able to sleep."

Though I try to not let his words affect me, I feel a softening in the center of my chest. To know that I brought him a small degree of peace in his hellish life, albeit unknowingly, makes me smile inwardly. The whole thing is insane, of course. Completely screwed up. But I can't help feeling a little pleasure at hearing his words.

What the fuck is wrong with me?

"After that, I visited your house nearly every night. Some nights, I'd find you still at work and I'd wait in the parking lot until you left. I told myself I was just making sure you got home safe. A girl like you shouldn't be walking home alone so late at night."

"Yeah, you never know what kind of creepy stalker may be following me," I say, my voice dripping with sarcasm. I'm not nearly so angry about the stalking as I am about his deliberate destruction of my family for the sake of his perverse desires.

He looks at me solemnly. "I'm not a nice man. I know that. I know I should have stayed away from you. I tried to just watch you from afar, but it wasn't enough. I had to have you. Had to know more about you. I'd see the way you'd laugh and smile with the other waitresses, or with your brother Jeremy, and I wanted you to look at me like that. I needed to see you smile at me with those clear, blue eyes of yours. I just… I wanted to know you better."

He pulls into his driveway before I next speak.

"So why didn't you just approach me and ask me out to dinner or something, instead of doing what you did?"

The look he gives me would break my heart if I wasn't so angry.

"Look at me. Can you honestly say you would have ever agreed to go out with me if you weren't forced into it?"

"Well, I guess we'll never know, will we? Because you decided to ruin my family and run us into debt with the Russian mob instead!"

He doesn't argue, doesn't try to stop me as I yell at him, pouring out all the hurt and betrayal. I knew he was a criminal, I knew he was bad news, but still I let myself fall for him.

When I finally run out of steam, he simply says, "You're right. I've done some terrible things in my life, but the worst is what I did to you. You didn't deserve it. I had no right to fuck with your life the way I did and take you against your will. Here."

He hands me a scrap of paper with an address scribbled on it, along with some other numbers.

"What's this?"

"It's the address for your family and the number for the account I set up for you. Go get your family and get them on a plane before the Italians find them. I didn't send my mom and sister away when I should have. I was too selfish. I can't take that chance with you."

I stare down at the paper, my body feeling strangely hollow.

"Go," he says more forcefully. "Get on a plane first thing tomorrow. Jeremy knows what to do. I prepped him when I first set them up. He'll have the number for my private plane and your new passports. You'll all have new identities. Go and start a new life. There's enough money in the offshore account I set up to keep you and your family comfortable for the rest of your lives."

"But, what about you?" Even though I'm angry with him, livid in fact, a small, pathetic part of me is devastated that he's letting me go. Which just goes to show how screwed up this whole situation is.

"You don't need someone like me in your life, Daisy. You're too good for that."

"Oh," I say in a small voice.

"And don't trust anyone," he says, face suddenly fierce. "I don't know who else is involved with the Italians."

"What do you mean?"

"The only way Nicky could have known about my part in Ray's debt is if he has an informant inside the Russians. You can't trust anyone."

"But you said they were all loyal. You said none of them would betray Ivan."

"I was wrong."

"But if they have someone on the inside, can't they get to you? They already shot you once—they could do it again!"

"Don't worry about me. I've faced worse."

My gaze traces the scars carved into his beautiful skin, and I want to weep. Yeah, he certainly has. And he faced it alone. Just like he's going to face this. Alone.

He's been alone for so long, the only way he thought he could convince someone to spend time with him was by tricking them.

"Just get on a plane and get on with the rest of your life," he says. "Leave all this shit behind." He hands me the keys to his sports car. "Go grab your stuff and leave. I need you safe."

I stand there, torn. How can I be so pissed at him, but so devastated that he's sending me away at the same time?

He's been messing with my head from the moment I laid eyes on him. I know what he did was wrong. It's so screwed up. I know that if my mom were to tell me that one of her boyfriends had stalked her, sent her spiraling into debt, then bought her at an auction to pay for that debt, the answer would be clear: run. Get as far away from him as you can. So why doesn't it seem clear now? How can I still want him, after what he did?

I can't think straight around him. I need to get away to clear my head.

I dart into the house and hastily throw my clothes into my bag. It only takes a minute since I didn't bring much. On my way back to the front door, I spot my small pistol still sitting on the table where I left it. I hesitate for only a moment before scooping it up and securing it in the ankle holster Dmitry got me.

When I get back to the car, Dmitry is still standing exactly where I left him. His blank, expressionless mask now in place, the same one he wore when we first met.

Part of me wants to go to him and wrap him in my arms, wants to kiss him until the mask falls away and I can see my Dmitry smile so gently and tenderly at me.

But I can't do that, because he was never really *my* Dmitry at all. Everything about our time together was a lie. He betrayed me, used me, lied to me. He put my family in danger.

He's no different than any of my mom's scum bag boyfriends.

And if I stayed, I'd be no different from her.

I climb into the car before I lose my nerve. As I start the car, I turn to him.

"What are you going to do?"

His gaze roams over my face as if committing it to memory. He reaches out to brush his thumb over my lip, but stops himself inches away. His hand balls into a fist and lowers back down to his side.

"I'm going to find the traitor. Don't worry, you won't hear from me again. I'm sorry I dragged you into this. You deserve better than a beast like me. Have a good life, Daisy."

Chapter 27

DMITRY

I watch the taillights disappear, a lead weight settling in my chest where my heart should be.

Heart? I snort, disgusted with myself. When have I ever had one of those? I'm nothing but an empty shell.

I stand there in the driveway for a long time, waiting, though I don't know what for. It's not as if she's going to turn around and come back. I've set her free. She's gone.

I head into the house to make some phone calls. I have to alert my pilot that Daisy will be needing him tomorrow morning, I have to tell Jeremy to keep an eye out for Daisy tonight, plus I still have some things to get in order for when they land in Argentina.

Pacing around the cabin as I make my calls, I'm suddenly struck with how quiet it is. How empty. When Daisy was here, there was a feeling of warmth in every room. Without her it's just… lonely.

The feeling puzzles me. I've been alone most of my life. It's what I'm used to. Loneliness has never bothered me much before. But now, the isolation feels foreign. Desolate.

I kick a chair in my dining room over just to hear the crash. The sound satisfies the churning emotions inside me. I pick up another and throw it across the room as hard as I can. It smashes into pieces against the far wall. I reach out blindly for the next item I can find and hurl that too. Furniture, books, sculptures; I demolish anything I can grab.

The house isn't silent anymore. Now it's filled with the satisfying sound of shattering glass and splintering wood. I roar as I lift the huge mahogany desk and slam it against the floor over and over, until it disintegrates into a shapeless pile of wood fragments. I whirl around, looking for something else to destroy when my gaze lands on Daisy's painting. I've seen her sitting here a few times working on this, but I never paid much attention to the actual picture.

She has beautifully captured the soft morning light and the serene atmosphere. But the person sleeping in the painting is a stranger. The high forehead, straight nose and square jaw look like mine, but the expression on my face is all wrong. She's softened the ugly, puckered scars crisscrossing my face and must have exaggerated the small, contented smile on my lips. There's no way I could have ever looked that peaceful.

I know what I look like. I'm frightening, ugly, and always a moment away from violence. I'm a beast. The complete opposite of the serene, sated, handsome man in this picture.

I reach out to tear it to shreds, but freeze before my fingers touch it. It's the last thing I have left of Daisy. Wrong though the image is, it's the last piece of her in my possession. As much as I want to destroy it, I can't.

My knees give out. I crumple to the floor, still staring up at the damning painting. That's the sort of man I should have been for her. That's the sort of man she deserves. But I can never be him. I've made too many mistakes in my life. Committed too many sins. All I can do for her now is stay the hell away.

I'm a curse. I ruin everything I touch. My mom, my sister; both dead because of me. Because I was too selfish to let them go. I can't let that happen to Daisy. She's better off without me. I've done nothing but bring her fear and pain and unimaginable danger.

I'll make sure she and her family want for nothing the rest of their lives. I'll give her the life she deserves, even if it's impossible for me to be a part of it now. Not after I lied to her the way I did. Betrayed her.

Only an animal like me could take someone as sweet and innocent as Daisy and crush her. I've bankrupt her family, forced her to sell her body, betrayed her love and trust, and now I've made her the target of the two most dangerous syndicates in the city. Both the Italians and the Russian traitor will be after her now. Her, specifically. Not just her family anymore. She'll be the target of every crook and criminal in the city, all because of me. Because the bastards know that I care about her.

That I love her.

Love is dangerous. It opens you up for pain. Gives others a means of destroying you. And because of me, because of who I am and what I do, my enemies will kill Daisy to destroy me.

Fuck them. I won't let them near her. I've already set her family up with more money than they will ever need. Now it's time to do what I do best. I'll hunt down our enemies and make sure none are left alive to ever come after her again.

Chapter 28

DAISY

I drive all afternoon and into the night, following Dmitry's directions to a small house out in the middle of upstate New York. As I pull up, the curtain in the living room twitches, then Jeremy comes bounding out of the house, relief written all over his face.

"Daisy! Thank God! Dmitry called and said you'd be showing up, but he didn't say what happened. Did you finally leave him?"

I shrug off his question and simply say, "We need to pack up now. Dmitry has a plane waiting to take us out of the country. Jer, he said you would know where the airport and our passports are?"

"Yeah, he told me about all that when he first set me and mom up. But why are we leaving now? What's happened?"

As he's talking, my mom comes out of the house and I quickly fill them both in on what's going on.

"So the Russians are still after us? Fat lot Dmitry did. He had the balls to buy you in exchange for them forgiving the debt, and they're coming after you anyway. What a scumbag."

"It's not Dmitry's fault," I snap. "He couldn't have known there was a mole in the organization. And it's not as if all the Russians are after me, just the ones who orchestrated Ivan's assassination attempt."

Jeremy looks at me strangely.

"What?"

"Nothing, I'm just surprised you're defending him. You *are* aware he bought you like a whore and raped you, right?"

"What?!" I shriek in outrage. "He didn't rape me! Everything we did was 100% consensual!"

"Oh, come on," he says, anger and disbelief at war in his voice. "You can't tell me you actually *wanted* to sleep with that animal? He's gone. You don't need to pretend anymore. It's just me, here. We'll get out of here before he can find us again. Fuck his private plane. I'll keep you safe from him this time. I know I screwed up before, but I won't make that mistake again. I'll keep you safe from now on."

His heartfelt speech cools some of my anger. "Oh Jer, I know you'll keep us safe. But I don't need you to protect me from Dmitry. He really isn't what you're making him out to be. He's actually a really great guy. You have no idea what he's really like."

My eyes sting, my chest aches with a hollow emptiness. Am I making the right choice?

Jeremy looks at me like I've lost my mind, but my mom is studying me closely.

My chest aches and my insides are like burning Jell-O — fiery and painful, yet oddly mushy and insubstantial at the same time. My skin feels like it's stretched too thin, like the tiniest bump could shatter me into a thousand pieces. I know that if either one of them brings Dmitry up again, I won't be able to stop myself from breaking down.

Thankfully, neither one mentions him again as we begin to pack up our meager belongings. We spend the night cleaning the house, removing every trace of ourselves, and catching what little sleep we can.

At nine thirty, Jeremy collects our passports, new IDs, and the money Dmitry gave him and hurries us out to the car.

"Come on," he says as we pile into the car. "It's only a twenty-minute drive. I called earlier and they said they're all ready for us."

My stomach is in knots the entire way. When we finally pull up to the airstrip, my heart is pounding like a drum and my forehead is sticky with perspiration.

This is it. This private jet is ready to whisk us away forever. Once I get on this plane, I'll never see Dmitry again.

I don't want to leave him, but what choice has he left me? If I go back to him now, I'll be no better than my mom. All those years that she stayed with horrible men, forgiving them for one awful transgression after another. I vowed long ago that I would never be like her. I would never let a man treat me like that.

Squaring my shoulders, I grip the handle of my suitcase and climb out of the car.

Chapter 29

DMITRY

I spend all night staring Daisy's painting, remembering every conversation with her, every touch, every smile. I replay the events a thousand different ways in my head. There are so many things I regret. So many things I could have done differently. Even from the beginning, Daisy never seemed bothered by my scars. What if I had just approached her? What if rather of stalking her home from the diner that night, I had instead gone up to her and asked her out for a drink? A cup of coffee?

She probably would have turned me down. But what if she didn't? What if she said yes? I could have gotten to know her the normal way. I wouldn't have had to resort to using Ray and the auction. Hell, if I had done it that way, I would never have had to agree to another six months, either. I'd be free of the Russian Mafia right now. I'd be free to take Daisy away, wherever she wanted to go, to start a new life somewhere else, with her.

The image of us laughing on a beach somewhere fades away, and I'm left staring up at that God damned picture.

The sun begins to rise, highlighting the soft, ethereal quality of the painting. I turn away in disgust.

It's too late. I can't change the past. I'll have to live with the decisions I made. I'll have to live knowing I betrayed the one person on this earth that I love.

I climb to my feet, my muscles stiff from staying in the same position most of the night.

It's a new day. Time to hunt.

All morning I travel around the city, quietly making inquiries. I talk to a few of my contacts who are friendly with the Italians, but so far nothing stands out as suspicious. At the top of my list of possible traitors is Josef. He's been intimately aware of the dealings I had regarding Daisy and Ray, since he handled much of the interactions himself. Since Nicky seemed to know all the details of that situation, it makes sense that Josef would have been the one to tell him.

As much as it makes sense, though, I don't want to believe it. He's as close to a friend as I've ever had. But if there's one thing I've learned over the years, it's that nobody can be trusted. Everyone always has their own agenda. You have to look out for number one.

After several hours of no results, I show up at Iniquity to question a few of the dancers there. While talking to one of the girls, I learn something interesting: apparently Raven, one of the regular dancers, just up and quit with no warning. It turns out she also called out sick for a few days, right before the hit went down. It's possible she got a tip about the hit and called out so she wouldn't be around when the bullets were flying. It's not likely, but it's more than I've had to go on so far.

She lives close to the club, so I swing by her apartment. But when I get there, Josef is already waiting outside her door.

"What the hell are you doing here?" I blurt out, shocked into an honest reaction. Shit, I need to play it cool. I have to keep myself under control. It never used to be a problem, keeping my emotions in check, but ever since Daisy…

Daisy. Just the thought of her name sends stab of pain through my chest. I was so close. She agreed to stay with me. She even said she loved me. And I fucked that up. She's probably on the plane right now, flying away from this hellhole. Disappearing from my life forever.

"D, you look like shit. What have you been up to?" Josef asks, looking calm and collected as usual.

"I've just been following up on some leads," I say, ignoring his first comment. If he is the traitor, the last thing I want is for him to know that Daisy is making her escape. "You hear anything new about Ivan's attack?"

"No, not yet. I've been following some of my own leads though."

I examine him carefully, looking for any trace of deceit. I don't see anything, he seems sincere, but that doesn't mean much. In our line of work, you learn how to lie convincingly.

"What brings you here?" I ask, still studying him.

"I heard from the other girls at Iniquity that Raven wasn't at work days before the attack," Josef says. "She might have known something. I figured it was worth checking out."

"Funny," I say. "That's the same reason I'm here."

"Yeah, well, if she was involved, I'm sure she's had enough sense to get out of town. I tried her here last night, and again this morning, but she's hasn't been back yet. I'll check with my contacts and see if she's hiding out somewhere in the city."

"You do that," I say. "Let me know if you hear anything. I'll go talk to the dancers again, see if any of them heard about her taking off somewhere."

Josef nods and walks off. As I watch him disappear, I can't help think how strange it is that Josef would show up here just after I learned about Raven's possible involvement. Maybe she does know something, after all.

If Josef is involved, and Raven knows it, it's just as likely she'd be hiding out from Josef as she would be from the rest of Ivan's outfit. If Josef is the traitor, he'd want to silence Raven before anyone else can get to her.

After Josef leaves, I head back toward the club intent on grilling the girls about Raven; any relatives she might have in the area, friends that might have taken her in, anything about her at all that might lead me to her whereabouts before Josef can find her.

As I'm walking down a narrow alley next to Raven's apartment, I hear footsteps from behind. They're very faint, barely audible. A normal person probably wouldn't even notice. But living as I do, it's enough to make anyone paranoid.

I keep walking at a steady pace, focusing my eyes straight ahead. I don't want them to know that I hear them.

There it is again. And not just one; three sets of footsteps. Well, at least they're making an effort to give me a challenge. Just as I go to turn the corner, the first man lunges out, as I knew he would.

I duck down, avoiding his tackle, and lash out with a quick jab to solar plexus. He drops to the ground, gasping for breath. I don't even have a moment to blink before the other two assailants are on me. I twist out of the second guy's grip and sweep his legs out from under him as I slam my elbow into the third one behind me. As they crash to the ground, I glance around to make sure that it's just the three.

When I'm satisfied there's no one else waiting to ambush me, I look more closely at the men. They're definitely Italian, with the standard dark hair and dark eyes. I remember these three from the basement yesterday where Daisy was being held.

I briefly wonder why they're not using their guns, but that thought flies out of my head as I focus on the fight. Three on one isn't much of a challenge for me, but it still requires my full attention if I want to avoid taking a blow.

I block a strike from the first guy I dropped and notice he already has two black eyes. I laugh to myself. It's the fucker who thought to lay his hands on Daisy. I would have thought he'd have learned his lesson yesterday, but apparently not.

I allow my lips to curl up into a small, mocking smile and wait for his move. He falls for the taunt, as I knew he would. He throws sloppy right, easily countered. I grab his arm and pull him into me, slamming my knee into his stomach in the process. As he's doubled over, I move in with a quick uppercut, landing it directly on his already broken nose. His howl of agony is music to my ears.

He thought the first black eyes hurt? Ha. There are many levels of pain. Cracking a freshly broken nose is relatively high on the pain spectrum.

When the second guy comes after me again, I pull a switchblade from my belt and ram it deep into his stomach. Shock flashes across his face before the pain even registers.

I twist the knife, smiling as he gasps in pain. He crumples to the ground, blood already soaking his shirt and spreading in a pool around him.

The first guy recovers enough to join the fight again just as the third guy attacks from the side. He actually manages to land a hit. It's only a glancing blow, barely felt, but it's the only one he'll get. I slash out with the blade in practiced motions. The one with the black eyes manages to jump back, avoiding the blade, but the other man doesn't notice it until it's jammed into his carotid artery. As I pull the knife free, his blood sprays out, painting the brick wall in a crimson mist.

I twist around to face the other two. The one with the stomach wound staggers to his feet, one hand holding his guts in, and stumbles away down the alley, but the guy with the black eyes and bleeding nose stands up and faces me as if he's unafraid.

"We're supposed to take you in alive. Nicky wanted you for himself. But, he'll just have to settle for your dead body."

His hand twitches towards his piece, but I'm already leaping forward. I grab his gun as soon as it clears the holster and thrust it upward. The shot rings out above our heads.

He gives a muffled curse as I wrap my fingers around his throat and squeeze. He tries to break free, but I have him pinned up against the wall, trapping him. I slam the hand with a gun against the wall a few times until his grip loosens and it clatters to the broken concrete. Thrashing for all he's worth, he attempts to kick out at me, but despite his size, he's no match for me. He's no match for a beast.

His face turns purple, and a memory floats up from when I had Viktor in a similar position. I had him pinned just like this against the wall of my living room. He also clawed uselessly at my hand, trying to free himself.

I let Viktor go then. The look of fear on Daisy's face then was enough to make me stop. But she's not here now. She'll never be here again. And part of that blame goes to this fucker right here. I may have shown Viktor mercy then, but this son-of-a-bitch went after Daisy. He will die.

I watch, emotionless, as his face turns from red to purple, then finally blue. His eyes roll back in his head, body going limp. I hold his lifeless body against the brick a moment longer before dropping him next to the dumpster in a pile of refuse. He doesn't deserve any better.

So much for Nicholas' promise yesterday. Despite his assurances about a truce, the Italians are still coming after us. Coming after me. I only hope I've gotten Daisy and her family away in time.

I briefly debate going back to find Nicholas and end him like I did his two goons here, but I refrain. He claimed he wanted peace with the Russians, but since he sent his men here out to take me, I can safely assume the truce is off. Instead, I head back home to do some sleuthing on the internet. If I can find where Raven disappeared to, I might be able to figure out who's behind this.

But when I get back to the cabin, I realize the computer won't be any use to me. It's nothing but a broken heap next to the desk I smashed last night. I take in the destruction around me for the first time, shocked at my complete lack of control last night. There are some sheets of paper peeking out of one the broken desk drawers and reach for them. My throat closes as I stare at the papers.

Daisy's sketches. She must have left them here. Despite my urgency to find the traitorous fucker, I sit down on the floor and stare at her pictures. She's drawn some new ones since I last saw them. One in particular makes my heart squeeze in my chest. It's a picture of us together, wrapped in each other's arms. I'm smiling at her in a way I've never seen myself do, and she's grinning up at me just as broadly. I remember this moment. It was right after I told her the truth about what I do. After she opened up to me about her own past. We laid there on the living room floor for hours after making love, just talking and laughing.

A wide, empty chasm opens before me as I think about spending the rest of my life without her in it. The thought of the empty years ahead drains the fight from me. What's the point? It'd be so much easier to just give up. Let the Italian bastards kill me, or the Russian traitor. What do I care, now that Daisy's gone?

But I can't. Not yet. Not until I'm sure Daisy is safe from all of them.

With that new determination, I head for the back door. The desktop may be trashed, but I keep a secure laptop locked in a safe under the shed floor. With that, I can hack into the city's street cameras and search for Raven at bus and Amtrak stations. It there's a trace of Raven anywhere in the city, I'll find it.

As I'm passing the kitchen, my cell rings. Josef's number flashes on the screen, but I silence it. He's called a few times earlier as well, and I ignored those too. I'm not in the mood to talk to anyone, especially him. Even if he isn't the traitor, I highly doubt that he found out any more information since this morning.

Leaving my phone on the kitchen counter, I head for the shed. Once there, I open the blinds around the room, letting the bright afternoon sun flood the space. Usually, the sight of all my carvings in here would fill me with a sense of pride and accomplishment, but looking at it now, all I feel is empty. Everything feels empty without Daisy.

A sound behind me breaks me out of my reverie. I whirl to face the intruder, but I'm too late. Pain erupts from my temple where the pistol butt hits me. I fall to the ground as if in slow motion, the world going dark around the edges of my vision. Viktor's gloating face is the last thing I see before it all fades to black.

Chapter 30

DAISY

We climb out of the car, my mom and I gathering our bags while Jeremy leaves to talk with the pilot.

"Mom?" I ask, the knot of tension in my stomach eating away at me. "I know I've judged you pretty harshly in the past for some of the men you've been with. But I wanted to ask…"

"Go on," she says when I hesitate.

"How do you know if the man you're with will turn out to be just like every other selfish loser you've ever been with? Are there any signs to look out for? How do you know when you're making a mistake?"

"Daisy, honey. I'm sorry to have to tell you, but most of the time you *don't* know whether things will go bad or not. Much of the time, you simply have to rely on luck and your own instincts. That being said, I know I've disappointed you and Jeremy over the years. I've made a lot of mistakes. After your father died, I was devastated. A huge hole opened inside me, and I tried to fill it anyway I could. I settled for less than I should have. When I think about how my bad decisions have affected you and Jeremy over the years…"

Her eyes tear up, her expression filled with shame and regret. She must be thinking about Mark, as I am. We never talk about him. It's a time in our past that we never, ever discuss. But the shame and guilt in her eyes now tell me she remembers what happened with him, just as I do.

"But in every relationship, I knew, even early on, that those men weren't right for me. Not one of those men ever put me first. I was never a priority with them. They were too selfish, and I was too lonely to care. It's my shame that I stayed with them despite that."

I feel my own eyes prick in response. I don't want to end up in the same type of relationship she's had over the years. If I go back to Dmitry, is that what I would be opening myself up to? Shame and regret for staying in a relationship I knew wasn't right?

"But you, you're different," she says, reading my expression. "You would never let a man treat you the way I've been treated. You have too much self-respect for that. I can see what you're feeling. You care about this Dmitry, and regardless of anything Jeremy or I tell you if you love him you need to follow your heart. I know you, and I know you would never care about someone unless he was worthy of it. You are so much stronger than I ever was. And if what you say about him is true, it sounds as if he truly cares about you. If you care about him too, then you need to fight for him. Don't let anger close your heart."

With her words, a feeling of freedom and lightness overtakes me. I know Dmitry did some really screwed up things. He planned and orchestrated the downfall of my entire family; he schemed to purchase me like one would a pet; he did everything in his power to trap me in his house forever.

But really, Dmitry isn't to blame for all of my family's problems. It wasn't uncommon for Ray to run us into debt. Yes, Dmitry encouraged him to borrow more than he usually would, but Dmitry was right. Ray was no good, and sooner or later he would have pushed us so far into debt that we couldn't hope to recover.

The fact that Dmitry encouraged Ray to send me to the auction is a bit harder for me to forgive. The humiliation and degradation that I felt standing up on that stage while those lecherous bastards leered at me; it was one of the worst moments of my life.

However, that, too, was my choice. Nobody forced me into Iniquity that night. I made that choice, fully understanding what I was getting myself into.

But as awful as that experience was, worse still was the night Dmitry was shot. The night I almost lost him. No matter how upset I am at him for the things he put me through, that pain is nothing compared to the devastation I feel at the idea of never seeing him again.

I can't stop thinking about all of the sweet moments between us. The nights I spent wrapped up in his strong arms, cradled by his powerful body. The moments when he dropped his guard, let me slip behind his walls and see the real him. The wonderful, protective, caring man he truly is.

I love him. Despite all his faults, despite all he's done to me, I still love him.

Though he made some bad decisions in the beginning, from the moment we met he has always put my needs and desires above his own. He waited to have sex until I was ready; he bought me sketch pads and paint when he saw my drawings; he taught me how to shoot and how to protect myself; he paid my family's debts, and even helped them flee the country to keep them safe; and in the end, he ultimately let me go in order to protect me. Time and time again, he put me first. Dmitry went out of his way to make me feel comfortable, to keep me safe, to make me happy. Hell, he's done more for me in the few short weeks I've known him than anyone has ever done for me in my life.

Despite my fears, I know, deep down, that he is nothing like the men my mom has dated. I won't be making her mistakes.

Dmitry loves me. And I love him. If I don't at least give us a chance, I will regret it for the rest of my life.

I can't get on this plane today. I'm going back for Dmitry. I won't give up on him. Not yet.

I hug my mom, tears in my eyes.

"I love you, Mom. Jeremy has all the paperwork. All the money. Everything you and Jeremy need to start a new life away from here. I'm going after Dmitry. We'll join you guys as soon as we can."

My mom squeezes me back and brushes the tears off my face. "I love you, Daisy. I hope this Dmitry does too. I hope he can deserve you."

"Come on, what's the holdup!" Jeremy yells from the passenger stairs of the plane.

"Don't worry, sweetie. I'll tell Jeremy. Just go, before he tries to stop you," she says, smiling through her tears.

I squeeze her hand, grinning back. "Thanks, Mom. I owe you one. I'll see you guys soon."

I dash around the car to the driver's side. Luckily, Jeremy left the keys in the ignition.

Jeremy looks confused at first, then desperate.

"No, no, no, Daisy! You can't be serious!"

I hit the gas, peeling out before he could reach the car and drag me out.

I speed down the highway, heart racing nearly as fast as the shiny sports car.

After hours of frenzied driving, the entrance to his driveway finally comes into view. I slow down, trying for the hundredth time to find the right words to say when I see him again.

On the side of the main road, close to Dmitry's driveway, are several unfamiliar cars.

Alarm spikes through me. I know for a fact there are no other homes on this particular street. What would these cars be doing here? If they were here to see Dmitry, why are they parked all the way on the main road instead of in front of his house?

There's only one reason that I can think of. Maybe it's the Italians, maybe it's the traitor, but either way, they aren't here for a friendly visit.

Leaving the car further up the road, I sneak through the woods to the house as quietly as I can. As I approach the house, I stop to listen, but I don't hear anyone inside. Dmitry's back-up car is still out front—he must be driving that now since he gave me his sports car.

I peak my head up over the windowsill to look inside. I gasp at what I see. It looks as if a bomb went off. I check window after window. It's the same in every room. Everything is destroyed, from the desk, to the dining room table and chairs, to the books on the shelves, even his beautiful sculptures—all of it a shattered wreck on the floor. Everything, that is, except my painting. It still sits there on the easel, exactly where I left it. It is the only untouched item in the entire house. How odd.

But even more disturbing than the mess is the emptiness. Dmitry isn't here. But where is he? And where are the men those cars belong to?

I'm over on the far side of the house now. There's only one more place I have yet to check. The shed. But just as I move around the corner of the house, I'm yanked from behind.

A strong arm wraps around my torso, while a hand clamps over my mouth, effectively silencing my shriek.

"What are you doing here?" A familiar voice growls in my ear.

Josef! Thank God. I spin to face him, but as I do, I go from relief to alarm. Dmitry warned me that there was a traitor. He told me not to trust anybody. That includes Josef. What if he's the one who sold him out to the Italians?

But these fears are put to rest by the first words out of his mouth.

"I'm here to help Dmitry," he says. "I think he's in trouble. I've been trying to call him for over an hour, but he hasn't been answering. I think I know who the traitor is."

"Who?" I ask. But before he can answer, we hear a loud thump from the direction of the back yard.

"The shed," I whisper.

Josef silently motions for me to follow him. Staying low, we work our way around to the other side of the house, the one closest to the shed. There's a moment of panic when we have to dart across the open space between the two buildings, but luckily no one is around to see us.

We creep around the back of the building, my heart racing out of my chest.

At least I haven't heard any gunshots yet, I try to console myself. As I think this, an image of Dmitry pops into my mind, pale, lifeless, and covered in blood. I have to bite my lip to keep from crying.

No, no, no, no. I can't let it end like this. Dmitry can't die like this, thinking that I despise him. Believing that I left him forever. I'd only just started dreaming of us sharing a life together. It can't be over before it's even started.

Josef is noticeably less affected than I am. He's the epitome of quiet determination. He easily slides his gun from the holster as he approaches one of the windows. I follow in his wake trying to step as quietly as possible.

As we get closer, we hear another dull thud. Then a grunt.

Luckily the shades are all opened. I quickly glance through the window, praying I won't be seen. Dmitry is tied to a wooden chair. I recognize it as one from the set Dmitry was making to replace his dining room ones. There are five men in suits, most of whom I don't recognize, but I can make out Viktor's snake-like smile easily enough.

"Viktor," I whisper so low it's almost a breath. "Viktor's the traitor."

Josef curses low. "I thought as much."

From my position at the window I have a perfect side view of the scene. If any of the men decided to glance in my direction they'd see me for sure. I know I should duck down and hide, but I can't. Because the dull thudding we've heard has now taken on a more rhythmic cadence. It's the sound of Viktor's fist slamming into Dmitry's face and body. I cover my mouth to hold in my gasp. Dmitry head snaps back with each impact. Blood coats Viktor's knuckles and his white collared shirt. His sleeves are rolled up to his elbows, his suit jacket is lying haphazardly on the table behind him.

"You always were a dumb fuck," Viktor taunts, a cold smile twisting his lips. "You swallowed every lie my father told you. Hell, you couldn't even figure out where the other half of Freddy's money went." He laughs coldly before delivering another punishing blow to Dmitry's jaw.

Josef joins me at the window, taking stock of the situation.

"You robbed your own family?" Dmitry says to him, spitting out a mouth full of blood. "What could you have possibly needed more money for?"

Viktor sneers and steps back, wiping his bloody knuckles off on a nearby rag. "You really think I had it that easy? You think my dad would just hand over the purse strings to me? I've been skimming off the top for years, and blaming it on the bookies. The best part is that then Ivan would send out grunts like you to punish the poor, innocent bastards!" He laughs uproariously for a moment before sobering once again. "But we both know who he really wants to take over the family business, and it sure as shit isn't his own flesh and blood. No. It's some dumb-fuck orphan he took in because he pitied him. A fucking grunt in the organization. The kicker though, is this dimwit is too fucking stupid to realize that the person who killed his whole family off and put him in the hospital to begin with is the same bastard who then took pity on him and brought him on to work for him!"

Next to me, Josef's jaw drops. I look back and forth between Josef's dumbfounded expression and Viktor's gloating face, trying to figure out what exactly he's talking about.

"Ivan didn't carve me up," Dmitry says. "Do you really think I wouldn't recognize the men who killed my family and cut into my flesh over and over and over again? You can't actually expect me to believe Ivan did that." Dmitry's voice drips with disdain.

"What is he doing?" I whisper to Josef. "Why is he taunting him?"

"He's trying to keep him talking. The longer Viktor talks, the more time Dmitry has before he's killed."

Viktor laughs, the cold sound grating on my nerves. "I didn't say Ivan did the dirty work himself, but he was responsible for it all the same. Your dumb-shit dad knew Ivan because he was a druggie and gambler. He owed Ivan hundreds of thousands of dollars and didn't have the money to pay.

"It was my first operation, did you know that? Ivan was finally starting to let me take on some new responsibilities. He was always, too weak with your family, though. He had a soft spot for your dad, because they went to school together or some shit. He only sent me there to scare him. But scaring him wouldn't have done anything. He still would've continued borrowing money that he couldn't pay, and Ivan probably would have kept lending it to him. We were at a precarious time with the Italians, still trying to solidify our foothold here. If we let a scumbag like your dad to get one over on us, it would have made us look weak.

"I had to protect Russian interest. I had to make an example of him. I ordered my men to go in there and do just that. It was on my orders that your family was murdered and their sniveling pathetic son cut up."

Dmitry lets out an inarticulate snarl.

"There's only one thing I regret about that night," Viktor continues, his eyes cold and ruthless. "That I didn't carve you up myself. How I would have loved to hear you scream. If I had

~ 226 ~

taken matters into my own hands that night instead of relying on others to do it, you never would have been left alive."

The coppery taste of blood fills my mouth and I realize I've been biting the inside of my cheek. I can't believe it. Viktor killed Dmitry's family? He's the one who had him mutilated? And this whole time, I just thought he was jealous that his father took him in as a child. But Viktor's sickness goes so far beyond childish jealousies. He's truly psychotic. Even as a teenager, he relished the idea of murdering an entire family and torturing a young child. He's sick. He's utterly and completely twisted.

"Because of my men's failure to kill you, I've had to spend my life staring at your hideous face. I knew that Ivan would be angry that I disobeyed his orders, but I figured he'd get over it when he saw the respect we got afterward. But that didn't happen. Instead, Ivan was furious. He had my men killed so one would be able to identify them, but worse still, he spread the rumor that the Italians were responsible for the kills. Stupid fucker. It's because of him that the Italians are so feared in the city. It was *my* kill. *I* should have gotten the credit!"

Viktor completely loses control. He descends on Dmitry again, furiously hitting him over and over. I cry out, but Josef quickly covers my mouth and pulls me down, out of sight. I sob silently into his chest while the horrible thuds continue on and one.

When they finally stop, the silence is even more awful.

Oh, God, please don't let Dmitry be dead. He can't be dead. But there are no sounds coming from the window above. No grunting or labored breathing or anything. Josef releases me and kneels up to check it out. I want to look too, but I'm terrified at what I'll see. I bite my hand to keep from whimpering as images of Dmitry's dead body flash before my eyes.

"It's okay, Daisy," Josef says. "He's alive. He's still alive."

My breath finally releases at those words, my lungs burning for air. I wipe my cheeks and kneel up next to Josef again.

Dmitry is still alive. Still conscious. But his face is a mess. Blood is everywhere, and his entire right side is swelling up. How can he still be conscious after that? How could anyone be?

"To make up for my 'over exuberance,' as he called it, Ivan took you in and paid all your bills," Viktor continues in a more normal voice, having regained control over himself. "In case you ever learned the truth about who was responsible for your family, he wanted to make sure that you would feel too indebted to him to ever seek revenge. His other reason was probably to punish me. He always bragged about you. Dmitry this, Dmitry that. He must have somehow thought that jealousy would keep me in line." He laughs. "That seemed to work real well, didn't it! And even now, over a decade later, he is *still* throwing you in my face, reminding me every day of my failure when I was nineteen. The only *failure* I had that night was not making sure you were dead. To this day, Ivan still refuses to listen to any of my plans! He's stuck in the old ways. He's always been too soft. Too weak. It's time for the younger generation to take over. It's time *I* lead the family."

Despite his injuries, Dmitry's bloody lips pull into a taunting smirk. "You think you can run The Syndicate better than Ivan? How? By bowing down to Italian demands? By conspiring with our enemies to assassinate your father? How would that help us? You're just announcing to every organization in the city that we're weak and ripe for take over."

"Oh, you poor idiot. Don't you see yet? The Italians aren't my enemies. Not anymore. Once we take out Ivan, we'll take out Nicholas too—you didn't think that senile old fool would have the wits to see the vision of my plan, did you?—and once he's is out of the picture, Nicky and I would magnanimously form a truce. One that would be very profitable to all parties involved."

"You and Nicky did all this just so you could get into the sex trafficking business?" Dmitry laughs a deep pained laugh. "Jesus, Viktor, I'm a scarred fucking beast and even I managed to land some pussy. What's your excuse?"

I cringe at Dmitry's crude language. Humiliation and doubt burn deep in my gut. Was I only just a good lay to him?

Then I see Viktor's expression, and terror chases my embarrassment away. Dmitry was just taunting him, again. Why? Why is he purposely riling Viktor up?

"He's trying to get him to kill him," Josef says, and the fear in his voice, the first I've heard of it, sends huge waves of alarm pulsing through me. "He's trying to piss him off enough that he'll kill him quickly, rather than dragging it out. Dmitry doesn't think anyone is coming for him."

Shit. I think he may be right.

Heat floods Viktor's face. He pulls out a wickedly sharp knife and holds it up to Dmitry's cheek.

"Oh yeah, we'll see how much pussy you get after I gift you a few more scars."

"Still more than you, I'd bet," he says with a smirk.

Oh, Jesus, Dmitry, would you just shut up! I think. *We're coming for you; just shut the hell up until we can get you out of there!*

"We need to do something," I say to Josef. "Can you take them out from here?"

"No," he says, his expression grim. "If I fire now, Viktor will slit his throat for sure. I need to draw him away from Dmitry first."

I'm moving before Josef realizes my plan. He tries to grab for me, but I've caught him by surprise. I'm at the shed door in a matter of seconds.

"No!" I yell, bursting inside.

Dmitry stares at me in horror. I've never seen him look so terrified.

"Daisy, what the fuck are you doing here!"

I ignore him, instead turning toward Viktor.

"Well, well, well. What do we have here?" Viktor laughs in manic delight before turning back to Dmitry. "It looks like you'll get to watch Daisy fuck me after all."

Immediately, two of the larger guards in the room step forward and grasp my upper arms, dragging me further into the shed.

"No, Jesus, Daisy, why didn't you get the fuck away when I told you to?!" Dmitry fights against the bindings holding him, screaming at Viktor in Russian. Though I don't understand any of the words, I can guess pretty well what he's saying. I want to tell Dmitry that it's okay, that we have a plan, but I can't risk tipping Viktor off. Besides, I don't actually *have* a plan, per se. I can only hope to occupy Viktor long enough for Josef to figure something out. But now, as I'm held securely by two of Viktor's men, I realize my mistake. Even though I've succeeded in distracting Viktor, now Josef has to worry about me, as well. If Josef makes a move, Viktor or his men could kill me in seconds. I just made his job that much more difficult. But I couldn't just sit by and watched while Viktor carved another chunk out of Dmitry. Not when I could have prevented it. Dmitry had no one to stand up for him when he was just a small boy. I'll be damned if I don't stand up for him now.

Viktor tosses the knife onto a nearby table and grabs me by the hair. Rough hands shove me to my knees. Viktor grins down at me with that cold, snake-like smile, the one I first saw on him that night at the auction.

"Come on Daisy. "Why don't you show me how you've been servicing Dmitry this past month? If you're nice, I may even fuck you before I kill you. How does that sound?"

Dmitry lets out a guttural roar and continues thrashing against the ropes. My heart's pounding so hard I can feel it in the tips of my fingers. Sweat breaks out on my brow, but I know I have to keep it together if I'm going to find a way to get us both out of this alive.

"Sure, Viktor," I say, making my voice soft and seductive. I cringe at the false flattery in it, but Viktor doesn't seem to notice. "I'll do whatever you want." I try to smile up at him but the expression wobbles on my lips.

"Of course you will. You're nothing but a little whore. I knew what you were from the moment I saw you. And now your little boyfriend is going to watch while you suck me off."

"Boyfriend?" I put as much disgust into my voice as I can. It's easy to do, looking up into Viktor's snake-like eyes as I am. "He's not my boyfriend. Why would I ever want animal like him? I only came here because he's holding my family hostage. I need to know where he's keeping them."

"Is that so?"

"I swear. You don't actually think I'd ever want a hideous monster like him? Look at him!"

Viktor throws a smirk over in Dmitry's direction. "Of course not. Who would?"

I smile up into his cold eyes.

"Tell you what: If you're a really good girl, maybe I'll force him to tell you where your family is before I kill him. Would you like to watch me carve him up and slit his throat? Maybe you'd even like to help?"

I have to swallow to keep bile from rising up in my throat before I answer. "Yes, please. He deserves it after what he did to me. Just, please help me find out where he's keeping my family first. I'll do whatever you want."

"You hear that, Beast. 'Whatever I want'." He smirks over at Dmitry as he begins unbuttoning his pants.

"Let's find out just how badly you want it," he says, staring down at me in greedy expectation.

I force myself not to flinch away at the sight of Viktor's hard cock that he's now stroking in front of my face.

Keeping my breaths as even as possible, I run one hand up his thigh, biting my lip seductively as I stare into his eyes. With my other hand, I surreptitiously glide down to the hem of my shirt, then further down my leg, moving slowly, carefully.

Dmitry furiously bellows, flinging more Russian curses at Viktor, who just smirks in delight.

I reach up and grasp Viktor's engorged cock in my hand, then lean forward, parting my lips as if to take it into my mouth.

Viktor closes his eyes in anticipation, his head falling back.

As soon as his eyes are closed, I grip the handle of the pistol and yank it out of my ankle holster. Before Viktor's bodyguards even blink, the gun goes off, the muzzle aimed right between Viktor's legs.

The sound is deafening. I'm immediately coated in dark, sticky blood. Viktor falls back with a roar. At the same time, the bodyguards pull their guns, one of them lashing out with a foot, knocking me back. The gun clatters out of my hands, skidding right past Dmitry's legs.

I hear a sharp crack and a blinding white-hot pain engulfs my right arm.

Another gun goes off, several shots fired in rapid succession. Two of the bodyguards fall to the ground, a crimson stain spreading across their creamy white shirts. The guard furthest to my left begins firing off shots in the direction of the window where Josef just fired from. The other guard lunges toward me. I raise my arms up to block my face, crying out in pain as my injured arm is unexpectedly jostled. Just before the man reaches me, another roar sounds from behind me.

Chapter 31

DMITRY

I watch in horror as Viktor shoves her to her knees. No. Please, God, no. She was supposed to be safe. I told her to leave. She was supposed to be safe from this.

Viktor grins at me in triumph. Daisy just gave Viktor everything he needs to break me. To well and truly break me. I attack the binds on my wrists with even more ferocity. I've been working on unknotting them since I first came to, but I'm not sure I'll be able to break free in time.

I watch Daisy hold back a flinch as Viktor threatens to force me to watch her suck him off. Then her mouth twists in disgust.

"Boyfriend?" she says in disdain. "He's not my boyfriend. Why would I ever want an animal like him?"

For a moment, doubt hits hard. Especially when she follows it up with, "You don't actually think I'd ever want a hideous monster like him? Look at him!"

Maybe she was only with me to save her family. Maybe everything she said to me was a lie. But then she smiles up sweetly at him and agrees to help 'carve me up', and that's when I know she's full of shit. No matter what I did to her or how much she hates me, the Daisy I know could never take pleasure in someone's torture, no matter how well deserved.

No, she's simply telling Viktor what he wants to hear. Clever girl. She playing for time, the same way I was. Maybe she has a plan. Please, God, let her have a plan.

But when I see her stroking Viktor's leg, I can't keep back my roar of fury. She's *mine!* Yet here she is, taking Viktor into her soft, delicate hand. Viktor will die for this. Nobody touches what's mine. He will fucking die.

Viktor closes eyes, letting his head fall back, and that's when she makes her move. Everyone in the room freezes in shock as Daisy unexpectedly draws out a pistol. The stupid fuckers didn't even search her.

My Daisy, so sweet and innocent looking, but with a core of tempered steel. Others underestimate her because of her innocent looks. But I knew, the first time I saw her, that she was made of stronger stuff

However, she's still only one person in a room with five other armed men, none of whom would hesitate to kill her. Even with her gun and the training I gave her, the odds aren't in her favor.

With a grunt of effort, I attack the knots binding me, and finally feel one pull loose. But it's too late. I was too slow.

Daisy's gun goes off. Blood erupts from between Viktor's legs. He screams and falls to the ground. One of the guards lashes out at Daisy with a vicious kick, sending her gun flying out of her hand just as another shot rings out. My heart stops as Daisy screams, grabbing her upper arm. She's been hit. Fuck!

Two more shots erupt from an unexpected direction. Frantically tearing the ropes from my wrists, I glimpse Josef's face disappearing behind the window sill.

Two of the guards drop to the ground, injured. Another one lunges for Daisy.

Desperate to get to her, I simply tackle him and snap his neck in one fluid motion. Josef fires again, winging the last guy in the shoulder. I scoop up the gun Daisy dropped and walk up to where he's now cowering on the ground, whimpering about his arm.

Staring down into his pleading eyes, I pull the trigger. Blood and brain matter explode across the floor. It's not enough. These fuckers touched Daisy. They *shot* her. It isn't enough. They need to pay.

I walk to the next fucker, groaning on the ground in a pool of blood. Josef got him dead center in the chest. He won't last much longer. I lift the muzzle and blow a hole through his head, sending the bastard to hell on *my* terms.

I do the same for the next fucker, and the next, taking out each target in cold fury, until only Viktor is left.

He's huddled on the ground, still crying about his mangled dick. We'll see how much he's crying when I put a bullet into every one of his major extremities, starting with his knee caps. A bullet to his head is too quick for him.

My finger tightens on the trigger, my vision narrowed until all I see is my target. Just before I pull the trigger, a sob brings me back to myself.

I turn to see Daisy standing against the wall, one hand wrapped around the bullet wound in her arm, her wide, frightened eyes watching me.

My lungs collapse, all the air whooshing out of me. She's here. She's really here, alive, though not unscathed.

I drop the gun and take a halting step towards her, willing her not to be afraid. She's just seen me for what I am: a killer.

But, amazingly, she isn't frightened of me. She stumbles over and collapses onto my chest.

"Dmitry. Oh, my God," she sobs. "You're okay. You're alive. I was so scared they were going to kill you."

I hush her, gathering her into my arms and squeezing tight. Her warm, slight body against mine reassures me that she's all right. That she's alive.

"Shhh," I hush her. "It's okay, Daisy. You're safe now. It's over."

But Viktor's moan of pain from the floor behind us contradicts me. It's not over yet. There's still one fucker left alive.

I'm barely aware of Josef strolling into the shed. All that matters right now is that Daisy is alive. That she's alive and in my arms, where she belongs.

"What are you doing here?" I growl into her hair, holding her close. "You're supposed to be on a plane. You were supposed to be safely away from me."

"I couldn't leave you, Dmitry. I had to come back."

"I never thought I would see you again." I tangle my fingers into her hair, holding her head more tightly against my chest. "I'm so sorry, baby. I'm so sorry. I never should have fucked with your life the way I did. I had no right. I should have walked away, should have just left you alone. I fucked up your whole life. I never should have interfered. God, Daisy. I'm so fucking sorry."

She laughs shakily and pulls away to look at me, tears clouding her beautiful eyes. "It's alright, Dmitry. I forgive you."

I stare at her dumbstruck. "Just like that, you forgive me?"

She gives me a watery smile. "Just like that. You never made me do anything I didn't want to. Yeah, you shouldn't have trapped my family into debt to get me into that auction, but if you had left me alone and walked away… well… I never would have met you. I never would have discovered what an amazing man you are. I never would have fallen in love with you. You went about it in a fucked-up way, I'll give you that. But even after you bought me, you never treated me like an object. You always put me first; my feelings, my safety, my happiness. Nobody in my life has ever done that before. Only you, Dmitry. I love you. Despite the way we met and the messed up things you did, I love you. Nothing will ever change that. I couldn't get on that plane today. Not without you. I want to spend the rest of my life with you."

I crush Daisy against me, my chest too tight for words. I bury my face into her hair, breathing in her scent, while my heart tries to pound out of my chest. She still loves me. It's incomprehensible to me, how she could still care for me after everything, but she does. She's here. She came back for me. Wetness gathers in my lashes. I bury my face further into her hair.

"I love you too, Daisy," I finally choke out. "Now that you're back, I'm never letting you go. I'll take you away from here, wherever you want to go. I'll make it up to you. I swear, I will. I'll do whatever I can to keep you safe and make you happy for the rest of our lives."

"I hate to interrupt such a tender moment," Josef's sarcastic voice breaks in. "But what do you want to do with this fuck-bag?" he asks, motioning to Viktor, still weeping on the floor.

My first urge is to tell Josef to kill him. If anyone deserves death, it's him. But I stop myself from giving the order. I know that Ivan would want the opportunity to hear this story straight from Viktor himself. And family or not, betrayal of this sort is not something Ivan will take lightly. I'd probably be doing Viktor a favor if I were to kill him now and spare him Ivan's wrath. But this shitbag doesn't deserve any favors.

"Leave him," I say. "Ivan will want to interrogate him himself. He'll want to handle this personally."

"Oh fuck," Viktor cries out, the first articulate words he's managed to string together. "She shot my junk off. She shot my fucking dick off!"

I walk over and glance down at him.

"It went through your thigh," I tell him after studying the wound. "Your dick is still there, more's the pity." I toss a towel down to him. He's crying and groaning, but my attention is averted by the squealing of tires out front.

"Josef, get Daisy out of here."

"No!" she protests. "I'm not leaving you!"

"Daisy, get the fuck out of here, now!"

Daisy looks mutinous.

"It's alright, D," Josef says. "I called the boss once I saw the cars down on the road. That's probably him."

Sure enough, Alec and Mikhail burst into the shed, two of Ivan's most loyal bodyguards.

I push Daisy's small body behind my own as they sweep the small space, weapons drawn. They view the four corpses dispassionately, zeroing in on Viktor's writhing form.

"What happened to him?"

"I shot him when he tried to rape my fiancé."

They nod, but behind me, I hear Daisy's soft gasp.

"Fiancé?"

Shit. Maybe I should have asked her first. But this isn't really the sort of moment I want her remembering when she thinks about my proposal. I'll wait until we're somewhere far away, on soft white beaches, before popping the question. One thing is certain: I am marrying this woman. She's mine. Forever.

Once Mikhail and Alec clear the room, Ivan enters, looking more haggard than ever. He sees Viktor floundering around on the floor and shakes his head in disgust.

"Get him in the car," he says in Russian to his men. "And get rid of those bodies." He turns to me with a look of apology as he takes in my battered face.

Until that moment, I've been so focused on making sure Daisy was okay that I've barely felt the damage, but now my jaw throbs and all the small cuts covering my face are beginning to sting, making their presence known. I pull Daisy out from behind me and hold her tight against my side. She hisses in pain when her arm is jostled. I need to get her away from here so I can stitch her up.

I wrap the towel more securely around her arm while I briefly recount the events of the day, explaining in detail Viktor's admission to working with Nicky.

Ivan looks unsurprised. "I had a feeling he was behind Freddy's theft, but I admit I wasn't aware of the breadth his duplicity had reached until just a few weeks ago, when he tried to have me killed."

"You knew he was behind your assassination attempt?"

"I suspected. He has always chafed at the restrictions I placed on him. It was only a matter of time before he rebelled. I had my men tracking him to find who else was involved. I am just sorry he brought trouble to you and your woman."

I lock gazes with Ivan, searching for any hint of deceit, but he seems genuinely remorseful. All these years, he has always appeared to care about me, yet if Viktor is to be believed, Ivan is responsible for murdering my family. I can't reconcile the man responsible for my family's hit and my torture with the man who has cared for me all these years. Was Viktor telling the truth earlier, or was he just trying to get a rise out of me? How well do I really know the man who raised me?

Before I leave here, I need to know the truth.

"Viktor said that you ordered the hit on my family, not the Italians."

Ivan sighs heavily. "Yes," he admits. "I did order Viktor to pay your family a visit. Your father owed money. I sent Viktor to collect it. But I never intended for him to take it so far. And I certainly never expected him to hurt you the way he did." Ivan meets my gaze, his own filled with guilt and regret. "When I heard about what he did, I took you in, paid your bills, and raised you as my own."

"And turned me into your pet assassin." The truth of this cuts more deeply than I expect. All these years, I thought I owed Ivan my life. I've done whatever he's asked; killed whoever he ordered. All in an attempt to repay him for taking me in the way he did. And all this time, he was the one responsible for what happened to me, to my family. He didn't give the orders to kill and torture, but he is the head of the organization. He should have known that Viktor would take it too far. Even back then, Viktor was a sick bastard. Ivan had to have known that.

"I have always thought of you as a son," he tells me. "And I want you to take my position, when the time comes."

"I'm sorry Ivan, but I can't do that."

Still standing nearby, Josef raises his eyebrows in surprise. To turn down such an offer may seem ludicrous to him, but I have no desire to live this kind of life anymore.

"I appreciate everything you've done for me over the years," I tell him. "But we're even now. I know I promised you another six months, but I've found the traitor, and the Italians are no longer an immediate threat. As far as I'm concerned, I more than repaid my debt to you."

Ivan is disappointed, but doesn't look surprised. "Still planning on opening your carpentry business?"

"Maybe," I say noncommittally. The less he knows about our plans, the better. He may seem fine now, but he might change his mind later on about letting us go. I don't want him to be able to come after us in the future.

"Well, good luck. I wish you two all the best. If you ever have second thoughts, you know that you are always welcome here."

I can only nod. After learning the part he played in my mom and sister's death, my feelings toward Ivan are all a jumble. I need time to sort it all out.

Turning to Josef, I slap him on the shoulder.

"Thanks for all your help. You saved Daisy's life."

"Don't mention it. You can owe me one," he says with a smirk.

"And I'm sorry I suspected you," I add. "I should have known better."

"Don't sweat it. I would have suspected me too if I was you. No hard feelings. You found yourself one very special woman," he says, nodding toward Daisy. "Take care of her."

"Oh, I intend to." My gaze locks on Daisy's. I can't wait to get her out of here. She's only been gone a short while, but it feels like an eternity. After we get out of here, she won't be leaving my side for a very long time.

She blushes at the dark, penetrating look I give her.

"So, that's it?" she asks, gaze flitting to Ivan and Josef, then back to mine. "We're free to go?"

"We're free." We stare at each other a moment longer, then I scoop her up and carry her out front to the car. "Let's get you stitched up, then go see your family," I say settling her into the passenger seat.

"Aren't you forgetting something?" she asks with a strange smile, her beautiful face flecked with drying blood.

"Forgetting something?"

"A question, maybe?"

I cock my head, still not understanding.

"Fiancé?"

"Ah…" Realization dawns.

"You *were* going to ask me this time, right? No tricks, no deals, no debts?" she says with a teasing lilt.

I sink to my knees there at the side on the car so her face is even with mine.

"No tricks. No deals. No debts. I *am* going to ask you. But not here, while you're still bleeding from a bullet in your shoulder and my face all busted up. I wanted to wait until we were away from here, somewhere beautiful, settled in our new home."

"Wherever you are is home," she says, laying her hand on my chest.

"I don't have a ring."

"We'll get one later. I don't want to wait. I want to begin our new lives here, now. Besides, we've never done anything conventional before, why start now?"

A smile tugs at my lips. "In that case…" I cover her hand with both of mine, keeping it pressed against my chest. "It's your choice. From now on, everything is your choice. I will never force you into anything ever again."

I take a deep breath, heart hammering with nerves. "Daisy, before I met you, my life was empty. Dark. Completely devoid of happiness or joy. But you brought light back into my life. After I met you, I began to hope again. Began to dream. I began to live. I love you. More than I ever thought possible. I need you in my life. If you'll have me, I'll spend the rest of my life protecting you. Making you happy. Taking care of you. Will you marry me?"

She reaches out and gently brushes my hair back from my forehead. "Dmitry, that's the sweetest thing anyone has ever said to me. But I don't need you to take care of me. I'm perfectly capable of taking care of myself. I've been doing it for a long time. What I want is for us to spend the rest of our lives taking care of *each other*. I love you, Dmitry. And I'd be honored to be your wife."

Epilogue

DAISY

6 months later…

"Daisy," my mom calls. "Have you finished any more beach paintings? We just received three more orders."

"I'll have them done by the end of the week," I call from the back room of the furniture shop, which Dmitry turned into my art studio.

After we settled down in Argentina with my family, Dmitry wasted no time opening up his own carpentry shop while I began taking art classes at the local university. Dmitry's handmade furniture and sculptures have been selling like crazy, as I knew they would. People come from all over the area to order his work. And soon after opening, Dmitry converted a portion of his shop into my own personal art studio where I create and sell paintings to the locals. To my great shock, my paintings have been steadily selling.

"Alright, then. I'll be taking off for the night," my mom calls. "See you in the morning."

I stand up and stretch my aching back. Dmitry appears in the doorway, an uncharacteristic frown on his face. His eyes trace the lines of my body, and the worry in his eyes transforms to heat. He steps close and rests his hand on my protruding belly.

"Don't push yourself too hard." Beneath the worry, love shines in his eyes as his fingers caressed my stomach. "I need both my girls healthy and strong."

I laugh, leaning into his strong chest and inhaling his distinctive, masculine scent.

"Don't worry. Your daughter and I are perfectly fine. You don't have anything to worry about."

To both of our surprise, it turns out that during our first week together, when my pills were still packed away in my bag at Iniquity, he had, in fact, gotten me pregnant. I was so nervous when I first found out. I wasn't sure how he'd react. If he even wanted to have kids or not. But his heartfelt joy and excitement were beyond all my wildest expectations. To say he was thrilled would be an understatement. He began working on furniture for the nursery as soon as he found out.

He smiles his special smile at me, and my heart squeezes at the sight. Since moving here, his smiles have become more frequent, but my reaction to them is the same as it was that first time I saw it, all those months ago. Looking at him now, it's hard to remember all the pain and weight he used to carry around with him.

Since we've left, he's been slowly coming to terms with the awful events of his childhood. He is still working on forgiving himself for all of the terrible things he did while working for Ivan, and there are some days when the memories of those he's hurt ride him hard.

When that happens, I let him know I'm here for him if he wants to talk. Sometimes he does, and I listen patiently and help him talk through the pain. Sometimes he doesn't talk, and those times I simply sit with him in silence, letting him know without words that I'm here for him. Always.

One of the first things Dmitry did when we settled here on the white sand beaches of Argentina was to set up funds for the families of those he's killed or maimed. It doesn't erase what he's done, but it helps ease his guilt, knowing that their families are taken care of.

Ivan has tried to contact Dmitry a couple times, but he wouldn't take the call. Though he still loves him and appreciates what he did for him growing up, I don't think he's quite ready to forgive him yet. And though Ivan isn't my favorite person, I do know that if it weren't for him, Dmitry probably wouldn't have survived. Maybe one day Dmitry will be ready to talk to him again, but for now he is content to carve his projects and lavish devotion on me and his unborn daughter.

My mom and brother live just down the road from us, and though Dmitry offered to pay for all of their living expenses, Jeremy refused. Jeremy insisted on taking care of our mom all by himself. He now works part-time for Dmitry, helping him run his shop, and spends his nights waiting tables in town. His boyish good looks net him plenty of tips, and combined with Dmitry's generous salary, he makes more than enough to pay for the small house him and our mom live in.

With Jeremy taking care of all of the bills, it isn't necessary for my mom to work. However, after years of working full-time my mom says she's bored to tears sitting home all day. She said she needs something to do or she'll go crazy, so she offered to help me out in my studio, dealing with customers and talking up my artwork to potential buyers. Her handling of the books and the customers frees me up to do what I love most, create. That, and spend as much time as possible with my loving, devoted husband. And pretty soon, we'll have another little addition to our growing family.

Dmitry says he wants to fill our house with children. I, on the other hand, think three is a good number. But we'll see what the future holds. There's nothing but possibilities ahead of us.

Dmitry pulls back, and I frown up at him.

"You're not going to run away on me again, are you?" I tease.

"Run away? Me? Never."

"You used to, you know," I say, staring up into his emerald eyes. "Those first few days in the cabin, you acted as if I was diseased. Every time I'd get close to you, you'd turn tail and run away. Were you that afraid of me?"

"I was terrified," he says, face completely serious. "You were everything I ever wanted, and everything I knew I could never deserve."

I brush his hair out of his eyes, caressing his beautiful, scarred cheek.

"Dmitry, you are everything I could ever want or need. I love you more every day. And our daughter is going to love you too. You're going to make an amazing father."

"Daisy," he says, resting his forehead against mine. "I don't know what I'd ever do without you. You're finally mine. And I am never letting you go."

His hands caress my shoulders, then lower. His mouth skims my collar bone, inhaling my scent. My shirt is slowly peeled away while my own arms reach for Dmitry's hard body.

Lifting me up onto the worktable behind me, he groans low in his throat, and proceeds to show me just how much I mean to him. He worships my body, proving to me that he will never, ever, let me go.

Notes from the Author

Thank you so much for reading Bought by the Beast! I hope you had as much fun reading this as I had writing it! If you enjoyed this book, I'd be very grateful if you'd post a short review on Amazon or your favorite book review site. Your support really does make a difference!

I am excited to announce that I have teamed up with Greg A. Russell to write the second book in the Wicked Dynasty series which will be available soon.

We would love to connect with readers and other authors, so don't hesitate to send us a message at WickedDynastySeries@gmail.com. Upon request you will receive a reply with a promocode for a free audio version of this book, Bought by the Beast (Wicked Dynasty 1), narrated by Nikki Monroe and Gregory Russell.

Do you want to continue on this journey with Josef's dark romance adventure? If so, here's a preview of Sold by the Siren (Wicked Dynasty 2):

Sold by the Siren

A Dark Romance (Wicked Dynasty Book 2)

Lexi Heart & Greg A. Russell

Marika

My family has been my world all my life. From swimming with my sister, my uncle's antics, and storytelling to writing songs for artists in my dad's music studio. Now that I'm an adult, it's time for me to move out, be on my own, and do the one thing my father has held me back from doing, sing. What I don't know when I sign a contract with a big-time music producer is who she really is and the kind of people she does business with. When one of those people, a big blonde man, storms into my life and makes my body sing, I have to learn how to contend with everything in this dangerous new world I've entered, including him.

Josef

Looking at my blonde hair and blue eyes, you wouldn't be able to see my scars. They're deep. So deep that I feel absolutely nothing when I'm inflicting physical scars on anyone who dares to cross me or the organization I'm next in line to take over, the Russian Mafia in Philadelphia, the Bratva. I don't feel anything anymore except the rush from making criminal deals or inflicting pain. That is, until I hear a song and see the one who sings it. She might have made a mistake entering my world and meeting with me, but now I'll do anything, including killing or dying myself, if it means keeping her safe and hearing her sing to me one last time.

Marika

The water is perfect this morning. I feel content and safe here, floating on my back, looking up at the clear blue sky. A hint of pine and other natural scents from the forest slightly tickle my nose as I breathe in the fresh air. Fish are jumping further out in the lake. Birds are flying around while squirrels are scurrying back and forth on the branches hanging out over the edge of the shore. The wildlife wouldn't be playing and watching me if there were any dangers nearby.

I'm singing the latest song I've written about a family living in a fishing village while the birds whistle along as my backup singers. I turn, reaching my arms out and kicking my legs, to swim a bit further out into the lake and sing the final lyrics.

The end of the song is both happy and sad. A child returns to a village once he becomes a young man. He misses being there and growing up with his loved ones. Another young family laughs together, kicking and splashing water at each other, and plays together while he watches them. The young man walks away, knowing he will return one day with a family of his own.

This lake is so hidden and out of the way that no one can hear me singing. It's fitting. My dad will only allow me to write and sell my songs to other artists he produces in his studio at our house. He's seen too many negative things happen to performers, including my mother. Now that we've moved on as much as we could, we have a good life with everything we need and more.

No one else comes to this area because of what supposedly happened at an abandoned house nearby. Ironically, it feels comfortable singing and swimming here because of the ghost story that arose from the incident. Supposedly a giant, scary man who lived in the house haunts these woods. The story goes that he was a serial killer. He kept a woman tied up in his woodshed, where he had carved up dozens of victims before her. She was able to get to one of his carving knives and cut herself free from her bonds. She then entered the man's house and used the knife to brutally stab him over and over until he was dead.

Enemies of the man came to the house to kill him, only to find the woman standing over his body. They told her that she denied them their prey and owed them something. They advanced on her, but she still had the knife and was able to fight them off and run outside. They caught up to her in the woods, then killed her and buried her body out here somewhere while leaving the killer's body to rot in the house. Now his scarred spirit is said to roam around searching for her.

We were speaking of the story at home one evening when my uncle told us another version of what happened. There was a big, scary, scarred man living in the now abandoned house, but his injuries had come from fighting while growing up as a gangster. He was a dangerous, scary-looking criminal with scars all over his face and body, but he was also a human being with feelings. He fell in love with a beautiful woman whose family owed a debt to other mobsters. The gangster hid her family in a safe place but brought her to his house. Though she wanted to be with her family, she agreed to be his captive and do whatever he wanted in return for keeping her loved ones safe. He would not touch her, though, not until she fell in love with him.

The mobsters who were after the young woman and her family did eventually catch up to them. They wanted to kill the gangster and take the young woman away to find out where her family was. She told them how happy she was that they were there to free her from such a monster and that she would get them the money her family owed. When they went to kill the gangster, she surprised them with a weapon she had hidden. The beautiful woman and beastly man she fell in love with stopped the mobsters together. They are said to be in hiding, living together safe and happy. A little research found that my uncle's version of the story was closer to the truth.

A little romantic adventure would be nice, but maybe without so much violence. I haven't been too interested in romance though, since Sven, my swim coach, came on to me a few years ago. He was also my sister Hanako's coach. I hadn't known that Sven was already sleeping with Honey; that's what we call Hanako.

Honey barged into the room while I was naked in Sven's arms, and she screamed. Luckily, we hadn't done anything but kiss until that point. The jerk suggested Honey stay, and the three of us have fun together. It was the only time I've used my Jiu-Jitsu training on a person. I can protect myself, but I hate violence, that's why my songs don't include any. I start to sing another song but reluctantly stop before I'm halfway through.

I should concentrate on my meeting scheduled for this afternoon instead of letting my thoughts wander. I'm not sure if I should tell my dad that I'm meeting with another music producer. He doesn't have to know about it at all unless it goes well for me.

A noise from the shore behind me, where all my clothes are, pulls me out of my thoughts. I turn, expecting to see deer that sometimes show up and watch me along with the other animals. I'm startled, and my heart is racing. A woman is standing there. She doesn't look scary wearing yoga pants and a sports bra. She's tall and pretty with a thick muscular body.

"Hello, I was running on the trail nearby and heard you singing. You sound so lovely," the woman calls out to me.

"Hello. Thank you. The water is great if you want to… Hey, wait! Wait!" I yell.

The woman is picking up my clothes and emptying the pockets onto the ground.

"No, stop!" I continue yelling.

She tucks my shorts and shirt under her arm, holds up and stretches out my panties, and laughs. I've never had any problems out here. I've never even seen anyone near here before.

"That's not funny!" I shout and begin to swim towards her. She turns and runs into the woods with my clothes, her maniacal laughter trailing behind.

It takes me a few minutes to reach the shore. I look around to see if anyone else is about before I get out of the water, completely naked. There's no sign of the practical joker. At least that jerk left my cell phone and trail shoes.

"Okay, you got me. Now please bring my clothes back!" I shout, turning my head to look into the woods. There's no response which makes me a little scared but more angry than anything else.

Continuing to yell into the woods while stepping into one of my shoes, I bend down to grab the lanyard attached to my cell phone from inside the other shoe. I look over my shoulder to make sure no one is behind me before retrieving my cell, then stop and quickly get over the feeling of embarrassment that someone might see me in such a position. But I wasn't comfortable with the view of my surroundings being obscured while bending over.

A routine of stretching exercises every morning has made me flexible enough to lift my knees, one at a time, and tie my laces to keep me from bending over again or sitting my bare butt on the ground or a log.

Today is the first time I'll be streaking unless skinny-dipping is considered streaking. A thought about using my cell-phone case to cover my privates comes to mind. The lanyard is not long enough and would probably look even sillier than my birthday suit. Instead, I wear it around my neck, allowing my phone to hang below my breasts. There was only a bit of change in my shorts' pockets, and I consider leaving it on the ground, but that would be littering. I pick it up and put it in the case while beginning to walk through the woods toward the trail.

There are sneaker tracks on the trail that lead in the opposite direction of my house. I hear voices. One sounds like the woman who took my clothes. The other is a deep voice, definitely male. I am tempted to go and get my stuff back even though I don't know if these people are dangerous, and I need to head home soon to get ready for my meeting.

The voices are getting louder. They're coming back in this direction. I move quickly behind a rock just off the trail. The brush hanging down covers me like it's a hunter's blind. I can see them coming through the openings in the vines and leaves: A gleam of light flashes in my eyes, causing me to blink. It's from the sun reflecting off a gold medallion hanging down from the man's neck. The sun also reflects off his golden blonde hair and his big muscles. He looks like he's been out running, like his friend, the clothes thief. He's wearing blue shorts and a white T-shirt. He is muscular, tall, and gorgeous.

"No, it's not funny!" he's chastising her. *Good!* "What if the girl calls the cops? You know what that could lead to. I just got the house and don't need the hassle right now."

"I'm sorry, Josef! But it really was funny. You should have seen the look on her face—Ouch!"

Did he just slap her in the back of her head? *Good!* He's handing her something that looks like a dollar bill. They're turning off the trail to head to the lake.

"Great! She left, and don't use that nickname outside of the city," he complains. I can't see them anymore, but I can hear them.

"Maybe she drowned. Ouch!"

"Let's bring her stuff back to the house. I'll try to see if I can find something that lets me know where she lives. Once she gets her things back, you will apologize."

"Yes, sir," she says with reluctance as I watch them pass by again. I'm not watching them as much as I'm watching him walk away. Darn! I could have just called out and told them to leave my clothes, but I was embarrassed. Well, more distracted. I'm not going to chase after them now. I need to get home.

The area around the lake has poor cell phone reception. I'll wait to call my uncle after I hike about a mile. That's where the reception signal gets better. I've told Uncle Suki about my morning swims at the lake, so someone knows where I am in case anything happens to me. That's how we got to talking about that house.

"Hello, Uncle Suki. Can you do me a big favor?"

"Hello, Mari. I would do just about anything for you. Just about. What is it?" my uncle answers.

"Please pack a bag with clothes for me. Leave it by the tree with Mom and Dad's initials carved in it, by the trailhead near our yard. Shorts and a T-shirt will be fine. Please don't ask about this right now. I'll explain later."

"All right," he says with a laugh. I can picture him shaking his head.

My uncle is a good man. He's a talent agent for many of the artists my dad produces. I thought about asking him to represent me. He does not totally agree with my dad's thinking, as he also represents artists produced by the woman I am meeting today. He would tell my dad about it, though.

A few more miles of hiking and there's the tree. A heart with the letters YY and JY is carved inside a heart on a Giant Wolf Oak tree. The pack is lying against the trunk where Uncle Suki left it. Thankfully, there is no one around. I'm not sure which of us would be more embarrassed if he saw me like this. There's a note on top of my clothes inside the pack:

Mari,

I hope everything is alright. I just found out that someone has moved into the gangster house. You may want to bring a bathing suit to swim over there from now on. I will see you later so you can tell me what happened unless it is something I don't want to hear.

Love you,

Uncle Suki

Maresuke, Uncle Suki, is my dad's younger brother. He lives with Dad, Honey, and me. Uncle Suki is sort of a combination of a second dad, older brother, and friend. He knows about my skinny dipping from a game of truth-or-dare we played with his now ex-girlfriend and her brother, with whom she tried to set me up. He was nice, but I still wasn't ready to date yet. She was nice too, but she wanted to get too serious too quickly for my uncle's taste. I put the clothes on and head into the house. I'll try to forget about the practical joker lady. The man's body with the sun glinting off of it may be harder to forget when I shower and get ready for my meeting.

Sold by the Siren will be available soon.

We hope you enjoy the entire series.

Remember to email us at

wickeddynastyseries@gmail.com

and request a promocode to listen to

Bought by the Beast (Wicked Dynasty book 1)

for free!

Thank you

Lexi Heart and Greg A. Russell

Made in United States
Orlando, FL
02 December 2023

40002445R00143